"I WANT A WARM COWBOY"

—hat, boots, tattoo, Coors belt buckle, and a room temperature IQ." Barbara laughed. "A Jim Bob."

Karen's eyebrows went up. "You know that's a stereotype."

"They must exist, though, or where'd the stereotype come from? I can see him now. Drives a clapped-out Dodge pickup with a gun rack. Has a dog named Bubba. Some uncomplicated guy with no worries, no future. Who likes to have a good time and doesn't make demands."

Karen grinned evilly. "Are you sure you want a, what was his name, Jim Bob?"

"A cowboy is every eastern woman's dream—slim, strong, stalwart, looking like the Marlboro man. Neckerchief and squint lines from studying the horizon, the western archetype. Someone who'll say, 'There, there, little lady.' "

Barbara felt decisive and focused for the first time in weeks. "That's what I'll do this summer. I'll go looking for Jim Bob."

Harper Monogram

LOVE WITH A WARM COWBOY

LENORE CARROLL

HarperPaperbacks
A Division of HarperCollinsPublishers

If you purchased this book without a cover, you should be aware that this book is stolen property. It was reported as "unsold and destroyed" to the publisher and neither the author nor the publisher has received any payment for this "stripped book."

This is a work of fiction. The characters, incidents, and dialogues are products of the author's imagination and are not to be construed as real. Any resemblance to actual events or persons, living or dead, is entirely coincidental.

HarperPaperbacks *A Division of* HarperCollins*Publishers*
10 East 53rd Street, New York, N.Y. 10022

Copyright © 1993 by Lenore Carroll
All rights reserved. No part of this book may be used or reproduced in any manner whatsoever without written permission of the publisher, except in the case of brief quotations embodied in critical articles and reviews. For information address HarperCollins*Publishers*, 10 East 53rd Street, New York, N.Y. 10022.

An earlier version by the author of pages 63–84 appeared as "Welcome Home" in *Kansas Stories 1989*, edited by James Girard. Topeka: The Woodley Memorial Press, 1989.

Pages 114–124 by the author appeared in a slightly different version as "Cowboy Blues" in *New Frontiers*, Vol. I, edited by Martin H. Greenberg and Bill Pronzini. New York: Tor Books, 1989.

Cover photography by Herman Estevez

First printing: February 1993

Printed in the United States of America

HarperPaperbacks, HarperMonogram, and colophon are trademarks of HarperCollins*Publishers*

10 9 8 7 6 5 4 3 2 1

To the Ucross Quintet
and the kind people of "Buffalo County"

1

Barbara Door gunned her car up the entrance ramp to I-435 where the highway curved around the south end of town. She shifted up and held her foot on the pedal until she was ten miles over the speed limit, cruising past the shopping malls and subdivisions, past Corporate Woods and the industrial parks, heading for the Kansas Turnpike west from Kansas City. Once beyond Lenexa, the buildings thinned out for glimpses of farms and pastures—open places. Then she drove past the orange barrels and onto the turnpike, past the last fringe suburbs. The horizon pulled back and the trees grew away from the highway and she got that one-hundred-and-eighty-degree look—big and green and open with the sky growing higher by the mile.

She had to get away. If she stayed in Kansas City, she'd drown in self-pity, stay depressed, be half ticked off all the time, blow her top or dissolve in tears at the least excuse. She couldn't sit still. She had to keep herself distracted from the hurt and humiliation.

The destination pulling her was a dude ranch in Wyoming, friends, a quiet summer. What pushed her out was complicated. She needed to be Elsewhere. The house would never stop needing repairs, there was always the next semester to prepare for, and the human contracts, however altered, remained.

Grimaldi, the bastard. He'd made sure they were altered. He'd lived with her for seven years, then he went on a Fulbright to Zagreb. He didn't tell her, didn't warn her, just came back and dumped it on her. Here's a little something from Yugoslavia. How could he do it, the son of a bitch? How could he hurt her like this?

When he came home and told her, she'd wanted to kill him.

Skimming the interstate on cruise control meant empty time to think or not, to listen to tapes or the radio, to eat out of a cooler at hot, windy Kansas rest stops, to drive till she was too tired to go on, then fall into immediate sleep at an anonymous motel.

Once out of the city, she settled into the interstate trance—that right-brained, nonsequential state where there was no logic and no analysis—shifting awake when traffic thickened, then lapsing back when the highway was clear.

The sun beat down and it was a hot shock each time she opened the car door and rose out of the air-conditioning at a rest stop where retirees walked their dogs around their RVs and stylish cross-country tourists in Hawaiian jams and L. L. Bean's best studied the Kansas map. Two bearded men and a woman with tattooed arms ate bologna sandwiches in the back of a battered VW van. Interstate democracy. If you've got wheels, you can go where you wish. She read the signs posted by the highway department beatifying Dwight Eisenhower as the Father of the Interstate Highway System (the better to transport arms, my dear) and studied the map as she spooned yogurt.

She felt sturdy and tough. She was going somewhere, alone. She rested, out of the glare of the sun and the vibration of the car for a few moments. She didn't want to stop until she reached Wyoming.

A honeymoon couple pulled into a parking space. The woman had been sitting so close to him as he drove that she exited on the driver's side. They held hands until they kissed good-bye to go to the separate rest rooms.

No kissing in public, thought Barb, it makes my heart hurt. What was wrong with my kisses, Grimaldi? I was good in bed, you said so. I'd try anything. Enthusiastically. Kept my figure so you'd want to. Why do I miss your going-out-the-door kisses? They were so casual, so much a part of the way we lived. I just took them for granted.

She got back into her car and turned on the loudest country station she could find. The horizon pushed back until it stretched, clean, like the summer before her. She drove past Salina, stopped to eat in Hays, then drove on—to the flat wheat fields, the barely rolling hills of western Kansas, where the wind rippled the dry grass like swells on the inland ocean. The long hours of scarcely changing scenery was the price she paid to get to the mountains.

She gave herself affirmations: You can take care of yourself. You don't have to act crazy. You are not a bad person. But positive thinking always segued into the accusing monologue.

You weren't fair, paisan, she told the imaginary Grimaldi. You should have given me some warning. You never said thank you. For a thousand broiled chickens, for two thousand loads of dirty clothes, for a hundred vacuum bags filled with dirt. What about the times you were sick? Who cared besides me? What about the times we fought? Nobody else gave a good damn except me and I cared enough to tell you when you were wrong so you wouldn't make a bloody fool of yourself. Is this any way to treat a lady?

She pulled onto the black gravel shoulder and turned off the ignition. When she got out of the car, the hot wind tried to push her east. She felt silly standing there, studying the curve of the wheat field to the fence line, crying, like a six-year-old whose baby doll had been taken away.

A few hours later she began to think of stopping—at Oakley or Colby. She was tired from packing and from driving, but most of all from separating—from saying good-bye and writing change-of-address cards and arranging to have the lawn mowed. Exhausted from having Grimaldi slip into her head every time she stopped concentrating. Something that hurt this much should have a more substantial name. "Jilted" sounded like a lover who didn't show up for a tea dance.

At home, trees sheltered her house, trees lined

the city streets. When she hit the interstate, they moved back to the edges of the highway right-of-way, then they moved back to cluster around farm buildings and stretch along creek bottoms. Now they had almost disappeared and the flat tableland murmured its subtle song of low rises and yellow fields until the earth curved away. Heat and grain dust and humidity hazed the hills and blurred the distances.

The grass rippled golden in the dry light. A few rainless clouds, so high she could barely see them, traced patterns on the limitless blue sky. She saw no people, no cattle, no buildings on either side, and only one car, miles ahead on the highway. In spite of discomfort and fatigue, in spite of the numbing drone of the car's wind rush, in spite of the confusion, suddenly the epiphany broke and she saw how much more beautiful the country was than any photograph. There was no frame on the open view. She breathed in the bigness of it. World without end. Beauty-blitzed.

The motel in Colby was cheap and clean, all she asked. She closed the curtain on the last of the light and turned the air conditioner to low and pulled back the thin chenille spread. She tried to avoid looking at the awful painting over the desk, dropped a Mozart concerto into her Walkman, and followed each note until she slept.

The next morning the sun was already blinding, but hadn't yet heated the high-plains wind, which whipped her hair around her face and made everything seem fresh.

At first it was blue clouds on the west horizon. Gradually the image cleared. The white was snow on the blue mountains. Then their outline became distinct, although it was hours before she'd reach Denver. She'd been miserable so long she didn't know any other feeling—but once she saw the mountains, her heart lifted for no good reason and the car seemed to drive itself.

She was headed for the Big Horns in northeastern Wyoming and decided to stop in Cheyenne rather than push on. It was five more hours at least and she didn't want to drive the unfamiliar mountain road to the guest ranch in the dark. She found another low-rent motel where the Indian manager interrupted his curry, wiping his mouth with a napkin as he came out to give her a key.

The next morning she ate at a chain restaurant and stared at men wearing cowboy boots and wondered if they were cowboys or rump-sprung truckers. She even saw a old man wearing a spotless straw Stetson. She was definitely getting Elsewhere.

Her jeans were streaked with car dirt because there was no way to get anything out of the hatch without getting dirty. She obsessed about washing the car all the way to Douglas, where she pulled off the interstate for lunch and found the Cowboy Carwash on the access road. One bay was wet, but the automatic changer returned her bill like a stuck-out tongue. She had coffee at a local restaurant, where the dark paneling was a relief from the glare outside. The log building, much painted, had a fireplace, exposed brick, and old, oak-framed mirrors.

Two old farts sat at the counter, and one young man with blue eyes. A tuft of sun-bleached hair stuck out of the back of his gimme cap. He wore scuffed boots and jeans that fit him like loose, blue lizard skin. She was afraid he'd catch her eye as she stared, so she concentrated on his wide, flat shoulders in the dip-yoke shirt and his lean back that tapered to a tight little butt.

"Is the carwash working?" she asked the motherly waitress whose generous frontage strained the polyester blouse.

"I'm sure it is," the waitress said. "I'll give you change when you leave."

Then Barb realized all this had been said in earshot of the blond cowboy. She had her city reaction: this creep will lie in wait for me at the Cowboy Carwash since he knows I'm going there. Come off it, Princess. You'd love to find him waiting for you at the Cowboy Carwash. It would give your ego a boost. He's cute, young, definitely healthy. Besides, whoever heard of a cowboy with AIDS?

She took a handful of quarters and headed back to the carwash. There he was, the blue-eyed cowboy from the restaurant, coming back empty-handed from the change machine. He looked at her and smiled. All he did was smile. She started to holler, "I've got change!" but he ducked his head and climbed in his pickup and drove away.

That felt good, as inconsequential as it was. Maybe she still had what it took. For the first time since Grimaldi came back from Yugoslavia she enjoyed a man's reaction. She started thinking about a cowboy, a warm cowboy. She called him Jim Bob.

She'd find somebody young and fun and energetic in Wyoming and have a good time. She'd find the John Wayne, apple-pie, American-flag cowboy looking clean-cut and acting polite. The dude lady's dream. It felt good just thinking about it.

She sped north on I-25 to Casper and dodged orange barrels. The natives say Casper is nine months of winter and three months of highway repairs. Casper Mountain faded back on her left. Now for the last, long stretch of bare, rounded Wyoming hills, as boring as Kansas, but browner. When she got out of the car at a rest stop, she didn't feel sticky with sweat. The sun was so bright it hurt, even with sunglasses, and she wished she had a hat.

She wanted the long drive to be over, but didn't want to get to Cloud Peaks. She would have to tell Karen, her friend who ran the ranch, what happened and she didn't think she could talk without going completely to pieces.

She turned off at Buffalo, drove through the town, and found Highway 16 rolling west through the foothills and into the Big Horns. She turned at Willow Creek campground, then wound up the mountain, through the trees, through parks and canyons, past ponds and reservoirs. The higher she went, the lighter she felt. The scenery was spectacularly beautiful, but she couldn't take it all in. When the asphalt road turned to red gravel, she checked the odometer. It was fourteen miles from the asphalt to Cloud Peaks and she was glad she had front-wheel drive, then she saw the Cloud Peaks sign hanging from the overhead crossbar of the ranch gate.

Karen met her with hugs at the parking lot.

"I'm so glad you're here," Karen said. Kirt,

Karen's husband, gave her a hug and they unloaded the car.

"I feel like I ought to pay you season rates," said Barb. Kirt put her bags in the tiny second bedroom.

"And therapist's rates, too," said Karen. "You can earn your keep. I have a few jobs in mind."

"Good. I won't feel like such a freeloader."

"Do you want something to eat?"

"Sure. Do you need to get back to work?"

Karen nodded.

"How are you and Kirt?" Barb asked.

"Better than we deserve. I didn't think I could love any man this long."

Barb knew there was more beneath Karen's flip remark.

They walked to the main building. She had a rough impression of log cabins scattered through the pines, a humming generator, and busy people. Karen led her around the huge stone fireplace in the main room of the lodge to the dining room, and someone put a plate of food in front of her. Afterward Karen suggested a nap. From eight hundred to eight thousand feet in three days was too much. She rested on the clean sheets in Karen's spare bedroom and looked out the window at hundred-foot pines climbing the mountainside.

She was Elsewhere.

2

The main room of the lodge was busy after dinner. Although no guests were in residence yet, the wranglers and girls had to get acquainted. They reminded Barbara of the kids she taught. They were college students, some were local ranch kids, and all of them were trying to save some money for the winter. She met the housekeeper, Doris, and her husband, George, who did maintenance. They worked at an Arizona guest ranch in the winters and came back to Cloud Peaks in May. The cook, a dour, blond kid barely out of high school, scarcely acknowledged her, but she met the head wrangler when he came in, hung his hat and duster on the pegs by the dining room, and walked over.

"You're Karen's friend."

She stuck out her hand. "Barbara Door."

"Tony Reinman."

Barb felt a rough, callused hand and saw a face with a broken-bent nose and gray-flecked brown

— 10 —

hair plastered to his forehead where his hat had rested. When he grinned, she saw a chipped eyetooth and he looked younger than he had before.

"How long're you staying?" he asked.

"All summer."

His smile grew. "When're you coming down for a ride?"

"Probably never," she answered. She assumed he was just being polite, but he looked disappointed. She explained, "I've never been around horses and I suspect I'm afraid of them."

"Well, come down and see what we do. The horses are all gentle. You won't be afraid."

"I understand that if you don't ride all the time, you get sore."

"I guess you do," he said, and smiled. "That's part of it."

"I can keep my seat. In the library. Saddle my students with homework. I can, uh, rein in unruly students, but I'm not tough enough to ride a horse."

Tony looked dazzled or maybe baffled.

"Besides," she admitted, "I don't know how."

"Nothing to it. I'll be glad to show you."

"Thanks. Maybe after I get settled."

Tony smiled again and nodded once. His boots were heavy on the bare floor and Barb wondered what he did all day with horses.

Kirt looked the part of the western host. His deep voice instructed the wranglers and joked with Tony. He looked like a real cowboy and dressed the part in jeans, flannel shirt, boots, and a red silk scarf. He was lean and fit enough to be a cowboy and bought, sold, and schooled the horses for the ranch. His silver hair hung to his collar and he had a regulation droop mustache and sleepy gray eyes. He just missed being really handsome. She wondered if single female guests were a problem. He grabbed Karen for a hug as she walked past him to sit with Barb. No wonder Karen was still in love.

The kids were clustered with Doris on the big, deep couches in front of the huge stone fireplace. She ran through the daily routine of cleaning, bed making, and kitchen duties for the girls. Kirt laid out the wranglers' chores, explaining about dude wrangling to the new hands. The conversation was laid-back and teasing and Barb could hear the banter and play in their voices.

Karen joined her in a quiet corner of the big main room—knotty-pine paneling and wide plank floors, small four-pane windows and benches along the walls, some decent paintings and a couple of stuffed heads. There were game tables and conversation areas, such as the one where they sat—two Naugahyde couches, a coffee table, and floor lamp around a well-used Navaho. It wasn't much for looks, but it was comfortable and nobody had to worry about damaging it. Barb thought the per diem was expensive, but Karen said she was naive. Cloud Peaks wasn't as expensive as some of the posher guest ranches. Families returned year after year.

"How're you doing?" Karen asked. They had known each other since college, where they were roommates, and there was real concern in her voice. During those years in Columbia, Missouri, they shared more with each other than they had with their sisters, or mothers, or boyfriends. They'd gone through so many things for the first time together—falling in love, getting through tough classes, learning the way the world wagged. Barb was the one who drove Karen to the doctor in the Kansas City suburb for an abortion when her boyfriend ran out on her. And held her when she cried those months afterward. Karen gave Barb her first joint, dried her tears when her First True Love turned sour. Barb remembered the night they dyed Karen's hair—a mistake. Karen got Barb through math classes. The hours in their room, the casual talk, the serious conversations, the hugs and tears bonded them, and when they got together, even after a long gap, time and distance flew away.

When Barb looked at Karen, she saw more silver in the blond hair, saw the signs of age around her eyes, remembered when she was a size eight, not twelve. But as they talked the new image and the old blended and she was Karen. Her fine fair hair was pulled back in a ponytail and her cheeks were pink from the high-altitude sun. Her green eyes studied Barb's face. Barb wondered if Karen was trying to bring her memories into the present.

"How am I doing?" Barb repeated. "Well, the altitude really hit me. I'll see if I can jog around the lake tomorrow."

"When are you going to work?"

Barb flinched. She hadn't looked at her Kate Chopin notes in weeks. "Soon," she promised.

"I mean, when are you going to work for me?"

"What do you want?" Barb asked, surprised.

"New brochure copy. Press releases. Feature story and a list of travel sections to send it to for next year. Quotes from printers. That kind of thing. Do you think you can handle it?"

"Sure. I just didn't expect . . ."

"Do you mind?"

"No. I'm pleased that you asked me. It'll make me feel useful, not so much of a freeloader. Let me see the old files tomorrow."

"Good," Karen said. She looked satisfied, a mother hen with one more chick accounted for. But there were still questions in her eyes. "So what else is new?"

Barb avoided looking at her. "I got a new course approved and on the class schedule. It only took two years. I got tenure this year. It was up or out."

"Congratulations, professor," Karen said, and raised her coffee mug.

"Associate professor." Barb returned the salute. She did feel good about that, now that the hassle of academic politics was over.

"Good times and bad times come at the same time," she said.

"What about the bad times?" Karen asked.

"I don't want to talk about it."

Karen didn't say anything. Barb owed her the story. She, of all people, needed to know what had happened, but it was just too painful to face.

"Maybe it would help if I talked about it," Barb said. "I could sort out the details that are bouncing around my brain. I told you Grimaldi came back from his Fulbright." Her voice started to wobble. "I'd tell you about what happened if I could play it back without going hysterical. I need to remember what happened, all of it, so that I can't forget the bad parts and lie about it later to myself. But not now."

A log snapped in the fireplace and Barb could hear the kids' talk from that direction. "So what do you want to do while you're out here, besides the writing?" Karen asked.

"Not sure," Barb said. "I've had it with sensitive, intelligent, civilized men. They are supportive, thoughtful, and caring—mostly about themselves. They have a sense of the tragedy of existence—and they're the central tragic figure in their personal drama. They make depression a life-style. They are intolerant of everyone's foibles, except their own." She stretched the tight muscles in her shoulders. "I need some time to put the pieces back together."

"This is a good place for that," said Karen.

Barb thought about the cowboy at the Douglas carwash, thought of that nice feeling when he smiled shyly at her and ducked his head. She thought of those shoulders.

"I want the opposite of Grimaldi. I want a warm cowboy—hat, boots, tattoo, Coors belt buckle, and room-temperature IQ." She laughed. "A Jim Bob."

Karen's eyebrows went up. "You know that is a stereotype."

"They must exist, though, or where'd the stereotype come from? I can see him now. Drives a clapped-out Dodge pickup with a gun rack. Has a dog named Bubba. Some uncomplicated guy with no worries, no future. Who likes to fuck a lot and have a good time and doesn't make any demands and doesn't dump his emotional shit on me."

"There might be one or two."

"Do I detect a note of doubt?"

"Are you sure this is what you want?" Karen looked concerned. "You just got loose from one cliché. Why pick up another?"

"Grimaldi a cliché?"

"Sure. Midwestern professorial, leather patches on the tweed jacket, wine and cheese, a Volvo sedan." Karen grinned evilly. "Are you sure you want a, what was his name, Jim Bob?"

"For the time being. A cowboy is every eastern woman's dream—slim, strong, stalwart, looking like the Marlboro man. A Platonic perhaps man. Neckerchief and squint lines from studying the far horizon, the western archetype. Someone who'll say, 'There, there, little lady.'"

"Good luck," said Karen, resigned. "You'll find a few, but you have to leave the ranch and go to town. Tag along to the Rocket Inn or the Outlaws Saloon Saturday night with the kids."

Barb felt decisive and focused for the first time in weeks. "That's what I'll do this summer. I'll go looking for Jim Bob."

Later she walked out of the lodge and down to the reservoir. The sun had dropped behind the mountains and the last of the amethyst light lingered, outlining them. Birds called her to watch the sunset. The stars were coming out, flung across the transparent, high-country sky. The water rippled silver on the lake and she could hear it lapping against the rocks of the shore. The smell of the pines floated over the water. The sounds from the lodge were faint.

She would have to face the world again but didn't feel up to it just yet. The ranch was her safety. It had taken all her energy just to get here and she couldn't take it all in. She didn't want to leave the clusters of cabins in the curve of the creek, which rushed cold and scintillant from another reservoir higher in the mountains.

The sounds were too clear, the air was too thin, the sun was too bright.

Grimaldi used to come to her office in the afternoon and announce, "They're putting on a great sunset and I've saved a place for you." She'd stop what she was doing, give him a serious kiss, then go to his office on the west side of the building and watch the sun go down behind the tree-softened line of the hills beyond campus. They would just stand together companionably and the tension of the day would evaporate in the golden light. She loved that moment. Now he'd ruined sunsets, ruined everything. She kept going to pieces.

She cried, standing there alone beside the mountain lake, watching the light show, thinking how much she'd miss the sunset alerts.

Then she heard Tony say, "Hi."

She turned and tried to smile, but couldn't. She wiped her face with her hand and said, "I'm sorry. I can't talk now."

3

Barb took Karen's advice and joined Tony and a group of kids when they drove to the tiny town of Big Horn that Saturday. She stood in the gravel parking area in front of the Outlaws Saloon and panicked.

I belong at a faculty tea, she thought. I belong at the opera. I belong at a gallery opening. I don't belong at a country tavern on a lonesome Saturday night. More than anything, I don't belong with a man who is doing his duty by a dude he just met and a bunch of wranglers and girls who probably think I'm Grandma Moses.

"Introduce me to some people," Barb said.

"Sure," said Tony. "Everybody's real friendly."

Barb panicked at the thought of having to meet a roomful of strangers, then told herself: This is ridiculous, Princess. You are a mature adult. You have faced rooms of recalcitrant undergraduates every

— 18 —

semester for ten years. You can muster the social necessities. Then why was she scared?

When she stepped inside, glittering eyes from twenty stuffed heads stared. She felt as though she were a prize mare, up before the judges.

"This here is Barb," said Tony to the bartender. "She's staying up at Cloud Peaks with Karen and Kirt."

Buzzy reached over the bar to shake and asked where she was from and welcomed her to Wyoming, hoped she liked it here. His red hair was thinning and his waist was thickening, but he looked like a man who had worked outdoors most of his life. He placed long-necked bottles on the bar in front of them and poured himself a cup of coffee.

The back bar was an elaborate mirrored affair she'd seen in dozens of cowboy movies. It looked a hundred years old, with a carved deer head in the center of the mahogany.

"How're Karen and Kirt doing this year?" asked Buzzy.

"Real fine," said Tony. "Much better than the couple that managed before." A look passed between them and Barb wondered what the previous managers were like.

"Karen and Kirt are good people," Buzzy agreed.

Barb swallowed a little Coors, gradually calmed down, and listened to Tony and Buzzy exchange news. Besides the staring heads on the walls there was the heroic version of the Battle of the Little Big Horn—Custer was still winning. Bird and horse paintings. Crowded between the heads were beer mirrors, antlers, skulls, announcements for rodeos,

Crazy Days, chamber music, a county fair, and an art exhibit. And framed photographs of people on horseback doing unmentionable things with ropes to cows. Barb had a kitsch attack. All that terrible stuff. She also knew snobbery was a defense. What if these people didn't like her? Well, people with such wretched taste, what could you expect? She studied the clientele—young men and girls, dude men and girls, and a couple of guys she couldn't quite categorize.

She didn't usually go to bars much at home because they were noisy and she liked to talk and listen. Then she remembered Grimaldi was gone and she should learn how to go to bars. That's why she was afraid. She would have to go out and meet people, make new friends, be rejected or accepted. Without the familiar supports or the comfort of her usual roles. She looked at herself in one of the beer mirrors. She looked strained, like someone had grabbed her face beneath the cheekbones and pinched. She looked like a schoolteacher dude lady—straight brown hair skinned back with a headband, minimal makeup, plain white shirt. Well, she was a dude schoolmarm. Maybe by the end of the summer she'd look different.

Tony was right—people were friendly and he must have known nearly everyone in the place. This was the social club for the kids who worked out on the ranches all week. They picked up the news and found out what was happening.

In spite of feeling uncomfortable Barb was able to make conversation with a teacher, a ranch hand, and a sculptor.

She gradually relaxed and caught a whiff of

something familiar. A girl arched her back, displaying upthrust breasts. A guy stood by the jukebox with one hand in his Levi's pocket, fingers angled toward the zipper, thumb hooked over the edge of the pocket. Another young man carefully recentered his hat, revealing biceps as he raised his arms. Tourists and dudes like Barb were just watching, but the local kids exchanged telling looks or casually brushed by each other in the crowded room. One girl with a perfect tush attracted covert glances as she maneuvered around the pool table.

Then Barb identified the atmosphere. It was the hormone miasma she felt rising from the undergraduates in her classrooms—a fog of longing and horniness. In class she was above all that, watching the children go through the inevitable dance. Here she would be a part of it.

What did she have to lose? Was she afraid she'd be rejected? In thirty-seven years she had plenty of rejection. Nothing that happened here could hurt as bad as Grimaldi's announcement. Was she afraid the department chairman would frown? That her academic colleagues would look down on the men here? Who cared if she hadn't verified their credentials, confirmed their degrees, approved their IQs? Forget that.

She threaded her way to the bar for another beer, then returned to sit with Tony and his friend Hal Simmons, a farrier. "What does a farrier do?" she asked. He was polite enough not to laugh.

"I shoe horses."

"Like a blacksmith?"

"No, they do all kinds of things. I just shoe horses."

"Do you have a shop?"

"Uh, no, I have a pickup and I go to the ranches."

"That makes more sense."

"Hal's coming up to Cloud Peaks next week to check our horses," said Tony.

"I've only had five days off since March first," said Hal. He sipped his beer. He was ordinary good-looking, nothing special, Barb thought, but he wore a Lacoste shirt and she couldn't help but notice his arms. Shoeing horses must be better than working out on Nautilus equipment.

"That count half days?" asked Tony, not impressed.

"If I have to drive somewhere to shoe a horse, that's a working day."

"It's your own fault you're so good. The big ranches call you."

"Yeah, they call once, then I don't hear from them and I don't know if they're going to call again, so I take on some more people, then they all want me the same day."

"You need a secretary," Barb said.

"Or a wife," said Hal.

"Oink."

"Thanks a lot," Hal said, disgusted.

"Where does it say, 'love, honor, do the books, and answer the phone'?" she asked.

"Around here you expect more from a woman." Hal had had a few beers, but wasn't hazy. Barb knew she was irritating him and something perverse kept her at it.

"Laundry service, housekeeping, childbearing, *and* secretarial?"

Hal shrugged and tossed back the rest of his Budweiser. "Girls around here don't mind."

"Tony is more diplomatic," Barb said. "He's the dude wrangler and has to keep a straight face when they ask funny questions. Makes allowances for dude dumbness." Implying that Hal didn't.

"He was always a slick-tongued rascal," Hal said. Tony shook his head and grinned, eyetooth visible. Barb felt tension between the men.

"You don't have to sweet-talk your clients?" she teased.

"The horses don't listen," Hal said. "But the owners are particular. I can't say anything about the horse or the previous farrier."

"Tony doesn't tell me about the other dudes, either."

"Well, his customers leave after a few weeks," said Hal. "I have to keep mine coming back."

Barb wondered if she had unintentionally pitted them against each other. Was her long-dormant flirting technique coming back? Hal turned away to talk to some other people and she was sorry she'd been sharp. She studied him. He was thirty, with a mustache, neatly combed hair, flat-bellied and slim-hipped in pressed jeans. When she shook Hal's hand, she felt the calluses. He looked like a real person, not a cliché cowboy, and she wanted to keep talking to him, but had turned him off.

Everybody put away what seemed like huge amounts of beer. Barb felt looped after two and stopped. The others kept drinking and got a little loose, but nobody seemed especially drunk. Maybe they were used to it, like the altitude.

They left about midnight and Tony got them back up the mountain without incident. There was giggling and soft talk from the kids in the back of the van.

Tony saw Barb to Karen's door, guiding her along the dark paths from the parking lot with one warm hand in hers. She had gotten out of the gray depression long enough to have a good time and the tension had loosened. Stars shone through the lodgepole pines and the air was chilly and fresh.

"If I had a place of my own, like my trailer at the Y-Bar, I'd ask you to come home with me," he said. He lifted Barb's hand and kissed it. She was touched at the courtly gesture.

"That's a shame you don't. I'd probably go. It's nice to know you'd like to." She surprised herself. It was always nice to know somebody found her attractive enough to take home. In spite of not being good enough for Grimaldi, in spite of gray in her hair and wrinkles around her eyes and a not quite perfect figure—a man thought she was attractive.

"Would you mind if I kissed you?" he asked, very shy.

She thought a moment, tried to read the look in his eyes, but it was too dark. Was he being polite or was he really interested? She shouldn't start anything she wasn't ready for. She should be more selective. She thought of Hal, the farrier, and his arms and his sharp answers and wondered if he would ask or just take. She shouldn't jump at the first invitation that came along, just because

Grimaldi had flensed her self-esteem and left her bleeding. She could list lots of reasons not to let herself feel anything. One or two, anyway. But she wanted that kiss. And didn't want to think about why.

She lifted his hand, still holding hers, and put it on her shoulder, then slid her arms around his neck and went for it. Her mouth was dry and she expected a shy little kiss, but he got serious real fast. She relaxed into it and enjoyed the sweet, familiar thing. When they broke for air, he nuzzled her neck and got her ear in his mouth. That made her crazy, so he kissed her again. She could feel herself getting warm. It felt normal to have her arms around a man's body, taste the sweetness of a kiss. Abstinence was strange. Since she wasn't about to go with Tony to the bunkhouse with five horny boys looking on, she reluctantly pulled away.

"Too bad this isn't the Y-Bar," she gasped.

"Maybe you could go for a ride with me," Tony said.

"Maybe." She fingered his scarf. "What did you have in mind?"

"Something more than just a riding lesson."

"I don't think I could do it on horseback."

"It's been done," he said, and they laughed.

"But I don't think I could." She stroked his cheek. "Be nice, though."

It was nice, but she didn't especially care about Tony. She was just using him to warm her ego. Maybe Grimaldi had killed that part of her that could care about people. Or maybe she was still licking her wounds. At least the old body responded.

The next morning Barb asked Karen about Tony.

"Tony's a good hand," Karen said. "Is he your Jim Bob?"

"Jim Bob wears his hat indoors, and a down vest. Pinball is his idea of an intellectual challenge. Tony is too bright and not nearly horny enough."

"He's shy."

"I wonder if Hal Simmons is shy."

"Find out next week when he comes up," said Karen.

4

Hal Simmons arrived Monday morning in his covered pickup full of arcane tools and set up his gas forge under a shade tree by the corral. Barb found an excuse to go down and stand around.

"What do you call this thing the anvil stands on?" she asked.

"A stand," Hal said. He was studying a row of heavy tools that hung from the side of the bench. He wore a white oxford-cloth button-down shirt and faded jeans and steel-toed high-top shoes, not boots.

"What's that?" she asked. It was a two-foot-high something of forged steel.

"It's a stand to put the horse's foot on," Hal replied. Besides the tools in the truck, there was an aerosol can of bug spray and several bottles of Gatorade.

Tony examined the foot of a horse tied to a corral post nearby. The cool morning sun filtered through the trees, made shadows in the delicate heavy-headed grass. The horses in the corral shook their bells and danced around, or ate from small metal troughs mounted on the fence. The other wranglers worked in the tack room or were out repairing fence. The first guests would arrive the next day and everyone was bustling around on last-minute chores. This was a resort that appeared to be a working ranch. People didn't lounge around a pool or play tennis; they rode or socialized in the lodge or went into the mountains to fish. The staff was busy, but not frantic. Something was always going on. It was the horses that made it different.

Hal selected a horseshoe from the dozens on a rack in the back of his truck and picked it up with a gripper-type tool.

"What's that?" Barb asked.

"Tongs," he replied. Then he picked up a hammer and grinned. "Hammer." His eyes teased.

"That one I could figure out for myself," she said, and grinned back.

He held the shoe in the blue glow of the propane forge and pumped a blackened leather bellows until a few inches of the shoe's metal curve glowed red. Then he took a wedge-point tool and made an indentation around the thick end of the shoe.

"That's a . . . ?"

"Swedge," he said. When he finished, he dipped the shoe in a thick wooden bucket of murky water, where it hissed and a curl of steam rose. He heated the shoe again, and when it was ready, he hammered it briefly, then took a tool that looked like an awl and punched holes in it. "Pritchel," he explained, "to make holes for the nails." Flattened shoe nails littered the bed of his truck.

Barb was hypnotized by the rhythm of the hammer on the shoe, each slow step of heating, hammering, and cooling, as the blank shoe grew to fit one horse's foot. Where the shoe was red, the iron was alive, as malleable as clay. Hal hammered and bits of slag flew around him. It seemed impossible that the delicate silver-gray flakes had come from the solid metal. Hal stood with knees slightly bent, the horse's foot resting on the stand, his short muleskin chaps protecting his legs. Sunlight through the trees scattered patterns on his stained hat and white shirt. Sweat already soaked down his spine and under his arms. Barb tried standing in the half squat he assumed, but her thigh muscles quivered after a few minutes.

Each blow of the hammer altered the shoe in ways too subtle for her to notice, but gradually, gradually, he shaped the shoes to his knowing specifications. At that moment he was powerful and elemental, bending solid iron, shaping it with fire and air and the hammer's clang. Vulcan in Levi's. She could have watched all day, but Tony tactfully led her away so Hal could get on with his work. Hal had thirty-five horses to check and planned to stay several days.

A man like Hal, who spent a lot of time outdoors, had a fresh look to his skin, thought Barb, that glaze of pink over the tan. Men who used their bodies looked different from men who sat at desks and pushed papers, even if the office men ran or biked or worked out. Outdoor men's eyes were used to looking farther than the office wall.

Barb went to her room in Karen's cabin and dragged the milk crate of Xeroxes and notes over to the desk. She plugged in the typewriter and dug some paper out of another box. She had promised the journal editor an article on Kate Chopin, an author who wrote local-color stories in the style of de Maupassant around the turn of the century. Chopin had published dozens of stories and several novels when her most famous novel, *The Awakening*, appeared in 1899. Horrified blue-nosed reviewers were savage in their criticism and Chopin apparently stopped writing. She died a few years later. Barb had a couple of ideas, mostly about the recurring theme of enlarged awareness—of awakening—the characters went through. She opened the folder and began reading through her notes.

The housekeeper kept the waitresses-cum-maids busy, George repaired winter's damage to the plumbing, the cook made a shopping list using the huge chopping board as a desk, the wranglers were doing something with horses, Karen was on the phone, and Kirt scouted, keeping track of everything. Barb felt sequestered and idle, compared with them. By lunchtime she had a much-scribbled-over outline. As long as she kept busy, she didn't scream at Grimaldi in her head.

Gradually the resort fell into place for her and she really saw the guest cabins. They were log and fake log, well maintained, with plain wood floors, simple sturdy furniture, and unit showers in the bathrooms. They were scattered down paths through the sparse, uncut grass and high pines, so that each seemed alone in the woods when actually they were within minutes of the main lodge.

Barb couldn't run around the reservoir at first, but had to walk and jog until she got used to the altitude. The clean air and the altitude and the constant splash of the creek were tranquilizers. Dry, high-country plants, with feathered, fernlike leaves and tiny yellow or blue flowers bloomed brilliant in the clear light. Scarlet paintbrush dotted the grass. She walked through musty-smelling yarrow and golden-hearted yellow daisies. When she looked up, she saw the curve of the mountain peaks serrated by the line of treetops. Sometimes the sun poured through a gap in the clouds as they moved over the Big Horn peaks and a patch of mountain or park in the distance glistened in the Bierstadt light. She and deer came face-to-face on the path to the salt lick and froze. A moose, on legs that looked too skinny for his body, visited the lick on cool mornings. His dark, velvety fur gleamed with red lights and he wiggled his big ears, then moved to the lake to snuffle and drink. Then he left to search for creek-watered willow leaves.

That night at dinner Barb questioned Hal about breaking and shoeing horses. Not only could he tell her what, he could explain why and how. He sounded half vet, half equine psychologist.

"I've grown up around horses. I don't have any trouble with them, but you have to know how to think like a horse, then be one step ahead of them."

Barb liked his masculine calm. His eyes teased and she was catching on that Wyoming men would just as soon tease you as give you the time of day. Hal spoke slowly and all of his movements were as rhythmic as his hammer on the iron. When Barb felt insecure or in a new situation, she got scared. "Be scared and do it anyway" was her motto. But Hal's easy, soft-spoken conversation and quiet answers slowed her down, so she didn't get anxiety-wired.

Tony asked Barb if she wanted to go riding after dinner. She hesitated because she wanted to keep listening to Hal, but he wandered off to a table of wranglers and seemed to be glad to be with them.

Barb tried to talk herself out of it, but she wanted contact with flesh to salve the places Grimaldi had left raw. She wanted the relief, she wanted to satisfy her curiosity, test her nerve. She wanted to do something that felt good. Tony followed her to Karen's cabin.

"How many hours do you spend on a horse in a day?" she asked as they walked the path. It was drizzling and the late twilight was fogged and silvery. In black hat, yellow gloves, and a waterproof canvas duster, Tony looked like a character in a spaghetti western.

"Couple of hours in the morning, another couple after lunch, depends on the guests."

"You must have a butt like iron," she blurted.

"It's flesh and bone," he said, and she could hear the grin in his voice.

She put on city boots and slipped a yellow plastic slicker over her jeans jacket and said, "Okay, I'm ready."

Tony shook his head. He untied his scarf, which turned out to be a square yard of yellow silk. He folded it in a triangle then twirled it and wrapped it around her neck. The scarf smelled like sweat and smoke and horse and man. That salty blend made her belly tighten. Remembered smells of Grimaldi and all the men she'd ever known intimately.

Tony grabbed a truly disgusting hat of Kirt's off the rack and jammed it on her head. Looking in the mirror by the door, she thought she looked like one of those hard-bitten pioneer women staring out of museum tintypes. She touched the soft, clinging scarf.

In the corral two horses stood saddled and coated with drizzle.

"Hold the reins and grab the mane," Tony instructed. Barb knew he must have said this hundreds of times, but there was no impatience. She followed his instructions and eventually was up.

"I hope this horse is dude broke," she said.

Tony grinned. His chipped eyetooth was growing on her. He gave her a few pointers, then they walked the horses across the park.

"There's a right way to do this and I'm not doing it."

"Turn your foot like this," he said.

She did and pain shot down her sciatic nerve from hip to ankle. She turned it back.

"You must get tired of telling guests the same things over and over," she said.

"I don't mind." He paused. "Sometimes it's funny."

"How funny?" She ducked low branches overhanging the path. She looked back and the cabins of Cloud Peaks faded like ghosts in the fog.

"The hands know the dudes aren't used to

horses, or the outdoors. It's our job to help them enjoy themselves."

"But there are a few laughs down in the bunkhouse afterward?"

"Yes," he admitted. "You wouldn't believe some of the things they ask. 'Mr. Wrangler, when do they plant the wildflowers?' 'When do the elk change into moose?' "

"Come on!"

"It's true," he said. " 'Mr. Wrangler, when do they put the bark on the trees? Does the river have a bottom?' "

"I don't believe it," she said, laughing.

"Naw. My favorite is: 'What kind of uniforms do the cattle guards wear?' "

They rode on through the trees. Moisture collected at the drooping ends of the pine needles.

"You must get tired of that," she said.

"No, I get to meet all kinds of people here. You learn about where they live and their work. You learn how small the world is."

This was not your cliché cowboy, thought Barb. Besides knowing about horses and guest ranching, he was sophisticated about people in a way she was not.

Along the trail sparse plants grew. Blue bell flowers hung delicately on hair-thin stems and she longed to kneel and see if they smelled as lovely as they looked. It was beautiful climbing up the trail, with rain falling through the trees, the horses' footfalls clattering on the rocks. Then reality intruded.

"My butt hurts," she said, trying not to whine.

"There's a place up ahead to turn around."

LOVE WITH A WARM COWBOY 35

The place was fifteen more minutes and by then her very bones were sore.

People did this for pleasure?

Tony dismounted and told her how to get down. He tied the reins to a tree and motioned her to follow him. There was no path and she dodged low branches. She wondered if this was some new and refined torture for dudes. Then they reached an open space. From a ledge over a canyon they could see water pouring off a shelf of rock. The spray rose and foamed in changing patterns of gray and blue and silver, rushing down with frightening force. She heard the deep roar of the falls and could almost feel the vibration. The air smelled different here—clean and piney—and she was caught. She had to hunker down and hold on to the ground. She wasn't afraid she'd fall; she was afraid she'd try to fly.

"It's beautiful," she whispered.

"Yes. It's hard to tell someone how beautiful it looks." They watched for a while, then Tony said, "Worth a sore behind?"

"No other way to get here?"

"No."

"I guess."

After a long time she stood up and Tony led her to a two-man tent back in the pines on almost level ground.

It had been a long time since she'd made love to anyone but Grimaldi and she was surprised at how hungry she was for the touch of this body. As she kissed him she started unbuttoning his duster. It took them a while to get the outer layers off, what with kissing and stroking, and they were damp from the drizzle by the time they shed the last bits of clothing. They stood there, and she ran her hands over his chest and around his back and embraced him so tightly he went a little off balance. His arms tightened around her and she kissed the curve of his shoulder. She felt tears start down her face, but they weren't tears of pain.

They crawled naked into the tent. There was a little padding under something furry and soft on the floor.

They groped and sighed. His butt, indeed, was flesh and bone. She felt she could never get enough contact with his warm, clean flesh. He was ready, but started doing things to her nipples so she could catch up with him. Tony was as expert at this as he was at wrangling. The shy seducer. The tent in the woods told her he might have done this before. At least he was resourceful. He came before she did, making funny whuffing noises, then he brought her off and she thrashed around and made even funnier noises. He fell asleep, snoring and legs twitching, for about five minutes.

"What is this?" she asked when he awoke. They were smoothing out the furry stuff.

"Buffalo hide."

"Great stuff."

Then he backed out of the tent and she heard him pee, then he stuck his head in and started with her feet and nibbled and kissed and licked his way up, lit the fuse, and the fireworks went off again. In fact, many times. He must have found a whole new erogenous zone.

When they had done all they could think of,

they just lay there. Barb couldn't have moved if the tent caught fire.

"We'd best go back while there's still some light," Tony said.

"Right."

It took three tries before she could sit up, then Tony helped her out of the tent.

She groaned as she dressed when she thought of the half-hour ride back.

"Can't I walk?" she whined.

"Put your mind on something nice."

This evening had been something nice and on the ride back she thought about all they had done. Her legs buckled when she dismounted and she collapsed in the muck by the hitch rail. Tony helped her up with no display of intimacy.

"I won't act like anything happened, around the lodge," he said. "But that won't mean it wasn't special."

"A true gentleman. Thanks. I'll try to behave myself, too."

Barb limped to the cabin. She hadn't thought of Grimaldi or felt sorry for herself for hours. Somewhere out by the waterfall the gray balloon of depression had vanished. She should have felt guilty about falling for the first warm cowboy who had asked her. She should have had some restraint and some care for what the people at Cloud Peaks might say. She should have waited, been more discriminating.

She "should have" lots of things. But she felt no guilt, and no regret. Her bones hurt, she smelled like horse shit, but she'd just made love outdoors with a strong, hungry cowboy. On a buffalo hide.

5

The next day Barb sat in the lodge waiting to go over brochure copy with Karen, who had greeted the first guests at breakfast, then turned them over to Tony for their ride. Then Karen and Kirt had gone off with George on some emergency in one of the unoccupied cabins. Kirt told Barb that Cloud Peaks was originally a hunting camp, then became a working ranch and the kitchen was added. Later cabins replaced the bunks that once lined the walls of the main lodge, and plumbing was installed. None of it had been designed to last fifty years and it needed constant repairs.

The heat from the fireplace made Barb drowsy. She couldn't believe she'd fallen under the spell of the all-powerful prick. That all she needed was a good— She couldn't believe she dissolved in Tony's arms. And she couldn't believe how good she felt this morning, except for the insides of her thighs, where sore muscles complained about yesterday's horseback ride. It wasn't just a boost for her self-esteem or a romp on the buffalo robe. It was contact with the rest of the human race. She had felt and touched and tasted and knew she was alive.

Then came Grimaldi's voice like a rough hand shaking her from a dream. "This isn't your style, Barb." She could see him sitting at his heaped-over desk in the study, gloom-shrouded, depressed. "You're not that kind, Barb. You're just using that cowboy. Come on. Who're you kidding, for Christ sake?"

Get lost, Grimaldi, Barb told the ghost. You can bother me, but you can't bring me down. I feel good and it cancels out all the hurt you gave me. I wasn't angry and I wasn't hurting out there by the waterfall.

Then it hit her—this was what Grimaldi's depressions were like. She had always tried to drag him out of his withdrawal. One year when the winter glooms lasted into spring, she'd said, "Let's go to New Mexico."

She'd written about the Santa Fe Trail and it was satisfying, after reading her way across it many times, to be there at the terminus—in the plaza that seemed too small for the history it held, at the church Willa Cather's archbishop had built.

"I'm not going to beg you to go out," she had said the third morning. Grimaldi's new broad-brimmed hat lay on the desk opposite the bed. "I'm mad as hell. Here I packed us up and did most of the driving and you're sitting here like a lump. Can't you at least make an effort?" She was disappointed and angry.

"I told you I didn't want to come. This was your idea."

"I'm trying to make you feel better so you won't be so depressed."

"How I feel has nothing to do with you," he said. His voice was flat and cold.

"Yes, it does. I feel like I'm living with someone embalmed alive when you're like this."

"I can't help it." He wore his tragic face and she knew that arguing wouldn't improve things.

"I'm going to the folklore museum and the other one near it on the east side of town. Then I'm going to the plaza for lunch. I may be back or I may walk around and look into the sales galleries."

"Have a nice time."

She had been angry the whole time. How dare he dampen her holiday? Why couldn't he snap out of it? She was helpless against his depression. And mad at herself. She didn't enjoy going around alone. There was no one to talk to, no one to make jokes with, no one to appreciate what she liked. She went back to the motel feeling out of sorts and still half-mad at him.

They had returned to Kansas City a day early.

Thinking back, she wondered if maybe Grimaldi really wanted to stay depressed, or had given up hope of escaping, or didn't know how.

Barb couldn't stand to be miserable very long.

Her way of escape wasn't AMA-approved, or Grimaldi-approved. Hell, even *she* didn't approve of it in the abstract. But it was effective. The depression had lifted. She liked men and she liked sex. She still felt shaky, but she felt better than she had since Grimaldi came back.

She stared into the fire's changing patterns, glad for a quiet moment in the lodge. It was scary that she could feel so good. That meant she could also feel bad. Not depressed bad, but new, risky bad. Tony was practically a stranger and she couldn't pretend that he meant very much to her. Tony was an AM country station on the car radio—he was just there and she hadn't made any effort. Hal Simmons, on the other hand, was intriguing. He seemed worth getting to know, like tracking down a special tape at the classical-music store.

He was patient with her ignorance, calm, and teasing. He didn't look like much—ordinary okay looking, slim-hipped and muscular, his battered brown hat screwed in place. Not tall; at five-ten they stood eye to eye. No deep, thrilling voice like Grimaldi, whose resonant baritone reading T. S. Eliot could raise goose bumps on a statue.

But when she looked at Hal, she got something back. She thought of his rough, scarred hands, with rings of black around the fingernails, and wondered how they would feel on her skin.

While she was sitting there Hal came in. She stood up and moved out of the fire's heat, embarrassed by what she'd been thinking.

"You go around to all the guest ranches and do this?" she asked.

"Guest ranches, any kind of ranches."

"What else?"

"Rodeos, polo games. Anywhere there's horses."

"Polo?"

"Every Sunday. This has always been polo country. The club was started in the 1890s, I think.

An Englishman, Bradford Brinton, settled in this part of Wyoming. They've turned his house into a museum."

"I didn't know that." There were lots of things she didn't know about Wyoming. She felt like one of her students—almost overwhelmed by what there was to learn. And like them, she didn't want it to show.

"I'll be at the Equestrian Club Sunday," he said. "Why don't you come?"

"I guess I could. I don't know if anyone else would want to go with me." The thought of going somewhere alone still scared her.

"Come anyway and I'll find you in the stands, when I'm not busy. You ask a lot of questions. Shows you're interested."

"I tell my students the only dumb question is the one you don't get answered." She thought a moment. "I've never seen a polo match. I thought you had to be humongously rich."

"Around here you have to have horses. Not always the same thing."

She studied his quiet face. "You're awfully nice most of the time," she said.

"Compared to what?" he asked.

"Compared to making derogatory statements and being a chauvinist."

"I'll watch it." Sharp, with no warmth in his voice. "And I'll try to ignore the pushy, feminist bullshit you put out."

She flushed. "That's how I learn, how I got to where I am."

"Which is where?"

"Associate professor, English department. When

your father worked on the line at the Leeds Chevy factory, that's important."

"Okay, Ms. Professor, but this is Buffalo County, Wyoming. You can be anything you like out here."

"Dependent? Passive?"

"No, no." He looked more amused than irritated. "Just take it easy and let men be men and you can be what you like." He grinned. "A dude. Or just yourself."

"I might try that last one if I could figure out who she is."

"Come to the polo games. The stands only hold about fifty people. Don't worry, I'll find you."

"Aggressive feminists never admit they worry." She was grinning, too.

6

Barb got lost and had to ask directions twice before she found the fish hatchery and, subsequently, the Equestrian Club grounds. She was nervous and scared that she had made a mistake. She wanted Hal to like her. She wanted to see what would happen between them.

Finally she found the small sign for the club, then a gravel drive to a building that looked like a depot. There was a shaded deck with café tables and chairs. Portable metal stands, mounted on an eighteen-wheel tractor, stood on the other side of the field. She drove over and parked. The refreshment stand was a coolerful of beer and soda and a big glass jar of bills.

People sat in cars pulled up in a line even with the stands, making their own box seats protected from the wind. Families, babies, teenagers, and grannies mixed easily. Except for a few Porsches and a Lincoln or two, it was hard to tell the richies from the horsies. She sat with a girl she'd met at the Outlaws bar the weekend before and tried to make sense out of the action on the field and the announcer's comments.

Polo looked a little like soccer with horses. The horses wore colored leg wraps; their tails were tied up and their manes trimmed. The players sat straight-backed, their mallets vertical between plays, their hats shading their faces. One team's shirts might not be identical, but they were all the same color, tucked into the white jodhpurs. The riders' knees were leather-padded and some wore western boots and some wore riding boots. They galloped over the watered, emerald grass of the field and she could hear the hoofbeats and players' shouts as they chased the tiny white ball for a chance to swing their mallets.

She saw everything with great clarity. Making mental notes kept her anxieties in check as she sat there, working on her squint lines in the brilliant sun.

It was a travel-brochure day with dazzling high-country light, the sky clear and blue until it met rain clouds working their way over the backdrop of the Big Horns. She could see the darker green of trees in every gully on the mountains. The huge playing field stretched flat and brilliantly green. In Wyoming they water constantly for what she thought of as "real grass"—thick bluegrass instead of the sparse bunchgrass or brome or whatever it was that grew on the brown hills. She looked, and sure enough, there was an irrigator-sprinkler pulled off to one side. The playing field was a lush oasis.

A game was in progress when she got there. The players' white jodhpurs stood out against their dark mounts, their loose shirts graceful as they moved in swift patterns against the grass. It was hard to see the ball, but she loved the graceful, powerful moves of the horses and riders, the mallet's circle as it sought the ball, the fast reaction as the players followed.

She fretted because Hal hadn't found her. She hated the uncertainty when she arranged to meet like this. Is the other person going to show up? Why is he late? What could have happened? Should she be angry, or was there some terrible accident? What did she do if he didn't show up?

Hal was right; there were only about fifty people in the bleachers. She wouldn't be hard to find. Actually she had come on her own, so she really couldn't say she'd been stood up. Maybe he was shoeing horses; that's what he was here for. Still, it made her jumpy wondering if he would show up. He was just another guy. This wasn't a real date. He was only a farrier. What did she care?

Barb had gone for another beer between chukkers—which were something like the quarters of a football game—when he came up and reached for a can himself. She caught her breath, then realized she had been holding it all afternoon.

Hal greeted friends, swigged half the can, and looked hard at her. He touched her pink peeling nose with one rough finger and said, "We've got to get you a hat."

"If I had a proper hat, would I fit in better?"

They walked to the stands. Sitting down, he was taller than she although they were the same height standing. Barb was longer in the leg; he was longer in the body. It felt nice having someone to be with after being on her own. He seemed pleased to be there with her, changed his beer to his other hand, and put his free one around her waist.

"What do you want to look like in your hat?" His eyes were warm. "Dale Evans?"

"Myself, I guess. A visitor who needs shade. I wouldn't look like a native no matter what I did."

"I'll work on it. What size?" He looked at her carefully.

"I don't know; small, I think."

They watched the play on the field for a while and then she said, "I hate to sound stupid. . . ."

"You are stupid," he said, offhand.

"Thanks a bunch," she snapped, and pulled away, but his arm stayed around her waist. That stung. Why should he, a farrier, for Christ sake, call her, Madame Professor, stupid? Where did he get off? Why did it hurt? Screw him. She watched the game in silence. Then she realized what he had done—given her a worst possible outcome. His arm was still around her waist, he hadn't walked away. Saying she was "stupid" freed her. Now she didn't have to make points by proving how intelligent she was, didn't have to be afraid he was judging her. Dumb was okay.

"Why'd you say that?" she asked.

"Once I've said it," he explained, "it doesn't make any difference whether it's true or not."

And it didn't.

"All right?" He squeezed.

"Yes. Amazing. How'd you learn that?"

He shrugged and studied her face. When he

looked toward the green field, his blue eyes pulled the green into them until they were both blue and green and she felt the ground tilt away.

She looked around. There was the relaxed air of a high-school football game. The announcer called plays over the PA and people wandered around, enjoying the day.

"If I don't ask some dumb questions, I'll never learn anything. The announcer is saying things I don't understand."

So Hal started pointing out what the players were doing and explaining about the "line"—players gallop in the same direction as the ball so they can't slam into each other at an angle. He also commented on the field—wet places where the horses stumbled. Then he told her about shoes. "Rim shoes are more forgiving," he said. "They let the horse slide. Heel shoes stick and the horse stops too fast."

She wasn't sure she understood, but it sounded reasonable.

"It must take a long time to train the horses," she said.

"Yes, and most of these horses are used every day, on ranches. Not just taken out for a run. So they're stronger than polo ponies they have other places. Wyoming horses are worth more. After a while"—he looked at her and grinned—"the horses know the rules."

She was almost able to follow the play when a rider took a spectacular spill, flying over his stumbling horse's head. Then the horse fell on him. The man lay on the grass and a murmur ran through the crowd. After what seemed like a long, tense time the rider sat up and was helped to his feet. He walked off the field to the spectators' cheers.

A few minutes later Hal was called over the PA and he excused himself. "Gotta go to work. I'll catch you later."

Before Barb could feel lonely, a motherly woman introduced herself and asked after Karen and Kirt. She was the angel of another guest ranch. If it ran in the red, she made up the difference. She lived most of the year in Westchester County, New York, but spent summers in Wyoming. She wore a simple cotton skirt, blouse, and windbreaker—all top quality—and sensible shoes. White hair set off a patrician profile—beaky nose, wide-set eyes, high cheekbones, and the actinic keratoses that Barb would develop eventually, despite sunscreen. Barb hoped she looked that good when she was that old.

"Was Hal explaining the game?" the woman asked.

"Yes. I can almost make sense of it. But why haven't they stopped? That was the fourth chukker."

"My dear, there are six chukkers of seven and a half minutes each." She took up the tutorial where Hal left off. "They have four minutes to tack up between chukkers, when they change horses." She assumed Barb was as interested as she and answered all questions without being patronizing. Soon Barb was even cheering in the right places. The older woman almost made Barb forget Hal had left.

After the last match Hal came back and they watched the steeplechase. She didn't care who won, but it was exciting to watch the horses gallop around the field on the grass track and arc over the wooden barriers, to feel the tension and hear people cheering. After they had tended to their horses, the players came to the clubhouse and the director gave silver plates to the winners.

Barb and Hal ate a buffet standing on the porch of the clubhouse. It was a big, open room inside, with a couch and chairs in one corner, oilcloth-covered tables, and folding chairs. Hal brought beers from the bar. The clouds, which had waited all afternoon, moved over the foothills and it started to rain. Everybody clustered indoors and Barb listened as Hal talked with his friends, catching up on news and discussing the games. She met polo players who wore cotton baseball hats with the club name embroidered over the bill. They were as friendly as the people in the Outlaws. Westerners were just less suspicious and more outgoing than folks back home, Barb decided. Nobody locked his car or house. They trusted each other.

People started to leave in the rain that made the grassless places around the clubhouse mud-slick. Barb found Hal and said, "Thanks for a wonderful day."

"Are you ready to go?"

"It looks like everybody else is leaving."

"I don't want this day to be over," he said, and stared at the wet field. His blue eyes pulled in its green.

"It's not over yet," she said.

"Come back to my place."

She couldn't breathe and felt dizzy. "Why don't we go someplace for a drink?" she stalled. He took her hand and held it. She looked in his eyes and couldn't find the bottom.

"Let's go to my place."

Then she had to decide. She tried to weigh the pros and cons, but she wasn't thinking too clearly. She couldn't breathe and felt light, as though she'd float away if she didn't hold on to something. This wasn't what she wanted. This wasn't some dumb cowboy with broad shoulders and a big dick. She didn't want to care about Jim Bob. For weeks she had only cared about how bad she felt. She didn't want to start anything where she was the needier partner, where she wanted and expected something. Was he just kind? Hungry? She couldn't sort out the answers, so she nodded and couldn't swallow.

He tried to give directions, but she couldn't grasp them. She got out a map, but dropped it. Then she dropped her keys. He laughed at her nervous clumsiness, then suggested she follow his pickup back to Story, a smaller town in the foothills halfway between Buffalo and Sheridan.

He drove the main road where Barb could see log houses set back in the woods, turned off on a gravel street, then pulled into a lot with sparse, unmowed grass, tangly bushes, and a hundred-foot spruce. The trailer was weatherproofed and redwood steps led to the door. She heard creek-trickling water nearby.

She expected some kind of blue-collar decor—Jim Beam bottles and plastic flowers. Instead she found a comfortable clutter, and surprisingly every spare foot of wall space filled with books on homemade shelves. On the way to the bedroom she noticed the living room was a spartan arrangement of sofa, chair, and TV. The kitchen was tidy except for breakfast dishes in the sink. One small room was his office and it was clear he needed a secretary. The other held a bed, table, and rocking chair.

"I'm scared," she said.

"Me too." He touched her peeling nose. "No need to rush into this."

"This could turn out awful instead of wonderful."

"I'll take that chance."

She felt as if she were thirteen and going to her first dance. She felt like Venus rising from the sea. She felt scared and happy and her hands shook when she lifted his hat off and smoothed his hair where it was pasted flat to his forehead. She moved toward him, but instead of kissing or embracing, just leaned into him. Then she buried her face in his neck. He smelled like sweat and horse and male. She groaned. He hugged her a long time without moving.

Then he took her by the shoulders and looked at her. His eyes were blue and huge. He kissed her and she kissed back and her knees felt loose. She started unbuttoning his shirt. She was okay until she got to the belt buckle, then she had to look down. "You undo this," she said.

She started to take her shirt off and he said, "Wait, I like to do this part." He unbuttoned and kissed as he went and she stood there, getting warmer. I've done this a hundred times, she thought. Why am I shaking? Why does this feel like the first time? She looked at him—naked, splendid. She pressed against him.

LOVE WITH A WARM COWBOY 53

"O-ho," he murmured. He cupped her bottom in his warm hands and said, "Nice, very nice."

She kept trying to breathe.

"You're shaking," he said. "Are you cold?"

"No," she murmured. She felt tears roll from the corners of her eyes.

She ran her fingers over his mustache and lips, across the cleft of his chin, and along the line of his jaw to his ear. She traced the whorls of his ear and leaned up to taste the lobe, rough velvet like the back of an elm leaf. She kissed the three moles that made a triangle on his shoulder and breathed the clean scent from the hollow of his collarbone. He bent and sucked one nipple, teasing it with his tongue. Her belly vibrated and the roof of her mouth itched. She cradled his head in her hands, felt his soft hair between her fingers. He straightened up.

She went hungry to his mouth and fed there. She could feel his chest on hers, his belly against hers. She pulled away, gasping, and he pushed her gently onto his bed.

She took his weight, solid and warm. He kissed his way down. She grabbed the headboard and groaned. When he stopped, she found his lips and felt him come home.

Time speeded up and they couldn't touch fast enough to find all the places they wanted to know. There was no bed and no trailer and no Story and no Wyoming. There was flesh and sensation and explosions of delight.

♦ ♦ ♦

They never even got the bedspread turned down. It was dark. Hal lay staring at the ceiling. She pushed pillows behind his head, then turned to nestle next to him, her head in the crook of his arm.

"How do you feel?" she asked.

"Mmmmm."

"Me too."

He lay motionless and solemn.

"Really, are you okay?" she asked.

"I feel focused, for the first time in a long time." He sounded replete.

"Good." She felt relaxed, for the first time in a long time. She turned so she could see his face. She traced the bone of his brow and ran her fingers down his straight nose.

"Does this bother you?" she asked.

"No."

Her fingers smoothed his forehead, ran over the ridge of a faint blue vein in his temple, touched the cheekbone. She brushed his mustache with the back of her finger. She wanted to memorize his face.

They lay there and she felt him drift into sleep. She dozed a little, then went to shower. A shower after making love was almost a way of prolonging it—watery afterplay. Every place on her body felt good and the water caressed it again.

"May I join you?"

She hadn't heard him come in.

"Sure."

Afterward he handed her a huge terry robe.

They sat on the couch and he offered to turn on the big television set.

"I prefer live entertainment," she said.

He laughed and said, "I guess you do."

Rain pelted the dark windows and she felt warm and dry and safe.

"I always thought intellectual ladies liked good conversation afterward," he said.

"Brain-damaged. All I know is, I want to do it again."

"Are you always this intense?"

"I don't know. Isn't it all right?" She twisted around in his arms to kiss him.

"Yes," he said. His mustache brushed her cheek. "Yes. That's the best thing about you. Well, the second best." He laughed softly and she giggled.

"Where are you working this week?" she asked.

"Hampton's, guest ranch northwest of Sheridan."

"Is that far?"

"Thirty miles?"

"Long way from Cloud Peaks."

"Not so far. I'll be out there Monday and Tuesday, maybe Wednesday. Why don't you phone here Wednesday night, see if I'm back?"

"All right."

She didn't want to leave, didn't want the day to come to an end, didn't want to drive that gravel road up the mountain in the dark. She wanted to keep the warm, whole feeling. She didn't want to think of having to make dates and arrangements. She didn't want to think about missing Hal when he was at Hampton's.

7

The next morning Karen stopped Barb as she walked through the lodge after breakfast. Karen held the phone to one ear and motioned her over to the desk. Barb waited till she hung up and scribbled a note.

"George can't fix the toilet in cabin eight without a part from town," Karen said. "And one of the girls has taken to her bunk and won't talk to anyone. Kirt and two of the wranglers are working on the footbridge and I'm waiting for a confirmation from a big party from Creve Coeur."

"What can I do?" asked Barb.

"This call was from my neighbor in Buffalo. She said there was a window broken and I'm afraid our house has been broken into. The summer rental people won't be there for another week, and I can't leave here today to check it out."

"Why don't I check your house and take George

LOVE WITH A WARM COWBOY 57

to the hardware store? I need to run an errand anyway."

"Would you?" Karen looked relieved. "I'll draw you a map to the house. And tell George you'll drive him to Buffalo."

"Why don't I talk to the girl? Which one is she?"

"Kelly, the one with the red hair. But you don't have to do this."

"I teach kids that age. I'm used to them."

Barb walked to the girls' bunkhouse, wondering what Kelly's problem was. Her period. No period. Boys. A particular boy. Maybe it had nothing to do with sex. Maybe it was bad news from home. College kids think of sex all the time. It had to be sex. Hell, she thought of sex all the time and she was thirty-seven.

She pushed the cabin door open and looked to see which lump of unmade bedclothes contained Kelly. She sat on the lower bunk opposite.

"What are you doing here?" Kelly said, with some hostility.

"Came to see what's on your mind."

Kelly hmmphed and rolled over, turning her back.

"Anything I can do?" Barb was used to surly kids. That's why parents sent them to college—to let someone else contend with them while they grew up a little. They were only in her classroom a few hours a week and she could enjoy them. They grabbed ideas like magnets and questioned everything. She taught them a little and they kept her on her toes. She watched them separate from their parents and grow.

"Just trying to help," Barb said.

"Drop dead."

More emphatic than expected. "Any particular reason?"

"Mind your own business," she said, muffled by the dingy quilt.

"I do my best. Have I stepped on your toes?"

Silence.

What have I done to tick off this nineteen-year-old girl? Barb wondered. I used my fork and didn't spit on the floor. I tried to be friendly with the girls and the guests, talked to the wranglers, and oh hell. Tony.

"Are you in love with Tony?" The direct approach unsettled them.

Silence.

"He's somebody special to be in love with," Barb said. "But I'm not in love with him."

Silence.

I'm in love with an idea, she thought. Jim Bob, the cowboy with the ground-in tan and dirt under his fingernails. Beer-can webbing on the floor of his pickup.

"Hey, lady," Barb said, raising her voice. "You got no competition from me."

Kelly rolled back over. If looks could kill, Barb would have stopped breathing.

"You're older and smarter and you took him away," she accused.

Barb saw Kelly's thick red hair, the glorious color of autumn leaves, tumble around her smooth cheeks. Her eyes, full of hurt, were red and teary. She was young and beautiful and healthy and intelligent and she was jealous of Barb, who thought herself aging and wrinkling and tired?

"Didn't know he belonged to you. I thought he was a free agent."

"He is," Kelly admitted. "I just wanted him to"—long pause—"be my boyfriend."

"Does he know this?" Barb asked.

"I've tried to be subtle," Kelly said, with some hauteur.

"Be direct, always best."

"He might not want me to—to be his girlfriend. I'd look like a fool."

"That's the risk you have to take. And I'd take it soon before he gets his tent down."

"What if he doesn't, if he won't? You know."

"Laugh it off. Pretend it doesn't hurt. Whatever works. Here." Barb pulled her out of the bunk. "Wash your pretty face and comb your hair. Catch Tony before he goes out with the guests this morning."

Kelly looked a picture of indecision. Barb grabbed her in a bear hug. "Do it."

"Okay. I hope I'm not making a fool of myself."

"If this is the worst thing that can happen, I guarantee you'll survive."

Kelly looked uncertain, but darted into the bathroom.

"Good luck," Barb called as she left. You could usually tell when a man was interested. Maybe wanting Tony so fiercely had interfered with Kelly's radar. She hoped she wasn't sending the girl to be rejected. Getting turned down at the beginning was not the worst thing.

Maybe getting turned down after seven years wasn't the worst thing, either.

Barb was talking to herself, calmly. She wasn't

screaming at Grimaldi inside her head. That was fading.

It hurt. But it was a new start. It was lonesome. She had to have someone who needed her or wanted her. She'd take care of them and they'd love her. She was still grabbing for someone because she didn't know how to be alone.

Karen's house in Buffalo had a newly broken window, but no sign that anything had been taken. George got a window glass and whatever the gizmo was for the toilet and they went back to Karen's where he replaced the pane. Karen's house was comfortable though sparsely furnished. She and Kirt put their money into horses. Kirt bought and sold horses for the guest ranch and kept theirs at Cloud Peaks for the summer. During the school year they both worked for the Buffalo School district—Kirt as an administrator and Karen teaching middle school.

Barb stopped at the drugstore on Main Street for sunblock, products of the Modess Corporation, and heavy-duty moisturizer. As an afterthought she picked up a pair of work gloves. The only hats were silly tourist straw hats, so she left without one.

By then they'd missed lunch, so she and George went to Colonel Bozeman's for the salad bar and luncheon special. Barb asked George to show her the Buffalo swimming pool, advertised as the biggest outdoor pool in the state. It lay gleaming and unpopulated at the foot of the hill in a park. It was still chilly for swimming.

When they got back, it was too late to face Kate Chopin and too early for supper. Barb drifted around, visiting with guests. One group met at the fireplace after their ride and talked about the weather, stock options, and new business ventures. Or was it venture capital? It sounded like an expense-account lunch. Barb was out of her element with the natives and with the dudes.

After dinner Sully, the young wrangler from Fort Collins, explained to Barb how he broke a horse. It sounded more complicated than obedience school and something like teaching—you had to make the horses/students think it was their idea. It would be great if Barb could find a way of sacking out literature students. With horses, you flapped a sack at them until they didn't get upset, then you could get the saddle blanket on them. Maybe if she flapped an illustrated, annotated *Moby Dick* at students, they'd get deconditioned to Melville and stop cringing.

Sully and the other wranglers wore broken-in jeans and western shirts and silk scarfs. Their boots were usually dirty and they wore chaps when they rode. Their hats weren't just for effect and Barb got used to seeing their hair flattened to their foreheads, which were paler than the rest of their faces. They smelled like fresh soap showers in the morning and horse by evening. It wasn't unpleasant and she got used to it, along with the leather smell from their saddles and boots.

By Wednesday evening she was twitchy. Hal should be back from Hampton's. She walked to the desk, then went back to stare at the fire. She wasn't worried. If he changed his mind, so what? He wasn't the only cowboy in Wyoming. He wasn't even that good-looking.

It's not working, Princess, she told herself. You do care. You want to phone Hal. You want to see him again. Hell, you want to drive to Story and tear off your clothes and get crazy again. You feel like Kelly—nineteen years old, insecure, not wanting to make a fool of yourself.

Finally she dialed Hal's number and there was no answer. Had he returned? Was he out doing something more important than phoning her. Was he just out?

"What's the problem?" asked Karen when she noticed Barb's anxiety.

"Trying to reach Hal Simmons."

"So that's where you disappeared Sunday night," Karen said. "Is Hal your Jim Bob?"

"No. He's too bright and sensitive."

"So what's the problem?" Karen cocked her head.

"I didn't plan to fall in love with anybody. I just wanted something simple."

"You ought to know it's never simple. He doesn't strike me as your type. What do you have in common? Besides the obvious."

"Nothing. I just like him a lot."

"I don't think this is smart."

"I feel like a teenager, having to go through everything for the first time, single again," Barb said.

"I thought you came to Wyoming to put yourself back together," Karen said. "Hal will take your mind off what you need to do."

"Maybe Hal is part of the cure," said Barb.

"That's too easy." Karen sounded irritated.

"Why do you have to have a man to 'cure' you? After getting rid of Grimaldi, I wouldn't get serious about anybody for a while."

"I didn't get rid of him. He dumped me. Hal won't trash me, at least not the way Grimaldi did. He can't."

"Have you noticed you never mention him by his first name?"

"Who?" Then Barb cringed. "No, I hadn't. Marty. Marty Grimaldi. His name was Marty and"—her voice wobbled with tears—"I thought he loved me."

"Maybe he did, as much as he was able," said Karen.

"It doesn't feel like it from here."

"When are you going to tell me what happened?" asked Karen. She wasn't demanding or merely curious. Barb knew she needed to know so she could understand.

"Have you got a few minutes?"

Karen nodded and they settled down in a corner of the main room.

"I never expected Zagreb to change everything, I won't say 'destroyed' because that's melodramatic, and I refuse to be destroyed by that scuzzbucket son of a bitch," Barb began. "We had been together seven years and I just figured it was the price of living with an academic. He was overdue for sabbatical. We'd appreciate each other more when he got back," said Barb.

At first there was silence, then she started getting long, chatty letters in envelopes with interesting stamps. He wrote about his two-room flat and the city and how he had trouble finding just the right yogurt and how they fried all the vegetables and it rained all the time. He talked about the students in a general way. They were going to produce one of his plays and he got involved with theater people. Barb didn't even pay attention to the names. She should have, when "Andrija" started showing up. One masochistic afternoon she reread all his letters from Zagreb in order. He mentioned Andrija more and more. Then suddenly there was no mention of her at all. Then there was a gap in the letters, then he wrote about his play and how it had gone. Then the letters got shorter and more impersonal. Barb knew something was going on, but didn't know what.

Barb remembered those months of unsatisfying letters—February, March, April—the winter of her puzzlement. Why hadn't she been able to see it coming? Why didn't she want to see it coming?

He was due back just before the end of the spring semester. After ten months she was eager and happy. They'd make love and talk and everything would be as it was before he left.

"I can remember some of it with absolute accuracy," Barb told Karen. "Some of it gets lost. Probably Grimaldi's version is different."

Grimaldi phoned and told her not to pick him up at the airport. Schedules were iffy and he could rent a car. She cleaned the house. She had a casserole in the oven and a bottle of wine on the table. She had actually gotten out the pink tablecloth and bought a bouquet of freesias and carnations.

When she heard a car in the driveway, she was happy he was back. She threw her arms around him and got a stiff hug and a cold kiss. She smelled airline booze on his breath and something else foreign and unfamiliar. His shoulders tensed under the tweed jacket and he didn't look at her. Barb didn't remember what they said. He paced around the living room, even went to the windows to check the yard. He looked around and she thought he was trying to get used to everything again. She hadn't changed anything. He went to his study and glanced in, then closed the door.

"Where are your bags?" Barb asked.

"There's something I have to tell you," he answered.

Barb got a weak feeling and sort of eased herself down on the couch. He was going to tell her he had an affair in Zagreb and she was going to have to be understanding and forgive him.

"This isn't easy for me, you know." He sounded defensive. "I met this woman in the theater department."

Barb braced herself.

"Andrija Mitevska. We worked together on my play. She's really quite good."

He paced behind the couch and Barb heard his footsteps now on the oak floor, now on the rug.

"We became. Very close."

Barb was mad as hell, but not surprised. She kept her mouth locked shut and waited.

"When the play was over, we kept seeing each other."

He really did seem to be suffering. Well, let him. It hadn't felt very good on her end, either.

"We got married in April," he said. "She came back with me."

"Time freezes here," Barb told Karen. She remembered him standing in the middle of the living room, the afternoon sun coming in the window, flooding the room with light. She remembered his jacket was wrinkled in back and his tie was crooked. She could smell the boeuf Catalan from the kitchen and hear Respighi on the FM station in the background. She remembered his voice, that practiced baritone that vibrated from somewhere near his diaphragm—apologetic and proud and sheepish and defensive and final. But she couldn't remember his face, or his expression. Maybe she wasn't looking at his face. Maybe it was in shadow.

"I just can't recall what he looked like that day," Barb said. "I was falling and a mountain was avalanching around me. I didn't even cry. I sat there unbelieving with this smothering weight in my chest."

When Grimaldi started talking again, he said something about not wanting to hurt her, but that it was inevitable. Barb must have nodded or answered, she didn't remember. She hurt so much she couldn't breathe and her heart pumped against her ribs. She must have started crying.

"Where is she?" Barb asked.

"I found an apartment out on Wornall. It'll do for us until we find a house."

The "us" he was talking about was them. Barb wasn't part of his life anymore and she couldn't believe it. He had ripped himself out of her guts and left her bleeding in shock. She was so numb she couldn't think. He ran out of explanations and rationalizations. Finally Barb stood up and said, "Congratulations. I hope you're both very happy." There was no sincerity in that statement, but at least there's a formula for what you can say in certain social situations and you don't have to mean it.

He looked at Barb and lifted his hands. She didn't know if he meant to turn palms out in a peace gesture or wring them in dramatic angst. After a moment he stuck his hands in his pockets and walked out the door. Barb wondered how she could feel so bad on a sunny spring day. She watched him back the rental car down the driveway. She turned the oven off and put the wine in the cupboard, then walked out the backdoor to her car.

She looked down the driveway. Tufts of crabgrass grew between the cracks in the concrete. It was chilly, even though the sun shone. She could smell earth and new green things. She could see the faint blue cloud of exhaust from the rental car. Through a row of university parking permits on her window she spotted Grimaldi's battered cowboy hat, the one he'd bought in New Mexico. When it had been his turn to drive, he wouldn't stop when she had to pee.

Barb stood in the driveway. She ran her hand across the windows on the driver's side of the car, then kicked the front door. She slammed her foot into the metal, feeling it dent. She changed feet and slam-kicked the backdoor. Then she raced to the front of the car. One foot on the bumper, then she was standing on the hood. She was panting and sweating. She jumped and landed flat-footed on the hood and heard the metal give. She jumped, grunting and panting, until her heels and the backs of her legs ached and the hood was bumpy and creased.

She couldn't see for the tears. She threw herself on the roof of the car and pounded, but it hurt her hands, so she stood on the roof and jumped and jumped, until she came down wrong and twisted her foot. She screamed, fell on her side on the car roof, and started to roll, but ran out of roof and lurched to the ground. One hip scraped the concrete and she felt the bite through her skirt. Her elbow hit the grass beside the driveway. She sat there panting, tears running down her face, moaning.

"I don't know how long I stayed there, but the sun went down and it got colder. I cried all night," she told Karen. "I wanted to phone somebody and I was ashamed to. As though it were my fault. I cried for the fun we had and for the good sex. I cried for all the training it had taken to get him to be a good roommate. I cried because I had been waiting for him and wanting him and looking forward to having him back. And he hadn't been wanting me."

Barb cried because it was a relief. She didn't want to admit that it was a relief to think of peaceful years of no seasonal depressions, no brooding silences, no weeks without conversation while he swam in the tragedy of his existence.

One moment she could see herself a jolly old lady, perfectly self-sufficient and happy to live alone. Then she thought of growing old alone, unloved, with no one to care if she got up in the morning or not. The neighbors would find her dead in a room stacked with old newspapers.

LOVE WITH A WARM COWBOY 69

That wasn't her real problem. She had been living alone for ten months. On hold. She could figure out a way to be an old lady. Alone, if necessary. What she couldn't face and couldn't even think about was how to live the next day, the next week, with her life pulled out from under her like a slippery Navaho rug. It was finding out there was no Santa Claus and the first time a date stands you up and missing the scholarship and the day your dog died and the dirt hitting the casket at your grandma's funeral.

All the plans, all the details of her life would change. She couldn't begin to take it all in. She would have to go to work. And face the humiliation when everybody learned what happened. She would probably have to meet Andrija. And smile. And see pity in the eyes of her friends and colleagues. And keep going, no matter how bad she felt. After all, she couldn't retire to a nunnery. This happened to people all the time, other people. She should be able to handle this, the same way she handled the ovarian cyst and the classes disapproved and the time Grimaldi came back three days late from the Modern Language Association convention.

Barb stopped and sipped the cold coffee. Her mouth had dried as she talked. Karen glanced at the activity around the fireplace. The wranglers were laughing at something Kirt said. Barb cleared her throat and continued.

8

The first person Barb had seen when she went to the office to check for mail was Dr. Wilkins, Barb told Karen.

"Great God Almighty, free at last," he said. "How about you and me, kid?" He grinned. He was at least sixty-three or four, thin and healthy, his silver hair combed smooth over the dome of his head, his eyes dancing behind the lenses of his spectacles. He was a bachelor, the only person of Barb's acquaintance she would call jolly. They sat together at faculty meetings because Barb enjoyed his company and he liked to break her up over his whispered puns. He was incorrigible.

That morning he knew the right thing to say. He wasn't exactly her mentor, but when it came to office politics, he was always in her corner.

"Thanks, I needed that," she said.

"Drop in my office if the going gets tough," he said.

Barb sat in her office and stared at the mail. She wanted to crawl into the kneehole of her desk, pull the covers over her head, and wait for it all to be over, but she had to meet a class in half an hour. She had been going through the motions for ten months while Marty was gone; that's what she would continue to do. She wouldn't glom on to anyone, or weep in public, or let anyone think she couldn't get along without him. Three weeks until "Grades Due" on her calendar. She'd keep going till then.

Grimaldi made an appointment to come to the house a few days after he moved into the apartment on Wornall with Andrija. Barb dressed with special care that night. Spent a long time on makeup, wanting to look in control, thinking how absurd it was. As though looking good, wearing a stylish dress, having hair and makeup just so would make a difference. If she wasn't doing it for him anymore, she must be doing it for herself.

She could have met him un-made-up, but that would be another statement, about nonconformity. She didn't want him to think she was too depressed to get herself together.

Nothing she could do, and nothing she could be, would make him stay. Not that she would take him back. She just wanted him to wish he hadn't left. She couldn't put on a more subservient personality the way she put on a new blouse. Stone helpless insecurity—even if she could look perfect and be the kind of woman he wanted and even if she threw herself one hundred percent into loving him, there was no guarantee that it would be enough this time or that it would be enough the next time another Andrija came along.

She thought of having a drink and rejected that. Even went to the kitchen for Valium, then put the bottle back on the shelf.

He arrived looking very casual and relaxed. His face was tanned and the Mediterranean nose hooked over his thin lips, kept his fine-boned face from being too delicate. He had just shaved the constant shadow of his beard. She knew by heart the ridge of his brow, the curve of his cheek, the cushion of his lips.

"What happened to your car?" he asked.

"Vandals."

"In this neighborhood?"

She shrugged. She wasn't real proud of what she'd done.

"I suppose you want to move your things out," she began.

"My papers and books."

"The clothes you didn't take with you." He'd gained a few pounds, probably because he was happy instead of tense.

"I'd like you to keep the house, if you want it," he said. "You can buy me out. I'll check with a lawyer."

"Thanks. You can take what you like. We bought most of it together."

"The San Ildefonso pottery? The Navaho rugs?"

LOVE WITH A WARM COWBOY 73

That gave Barb a moment of indecision.

"Hell, take them," he said.

She remembered the trips to Santa Fe and the fun they usually had. "I'll trade you the pots and baskets for the rugs," she offered.

"Deal."

"What else do we have to settle?"

He didn't say anything. He was pacing around the living room, appraising it for real-estate purposes, she supposed.

"I didn't expect you to take it so well," he said.

"I'm not taking it well."

"You're not making a fuss."

"I'm too numb."

She looked at him and wondered that she ever thought she knew him. Feeling in tune with him had attracted her in the first place. Had she ever really known him?

She should have been able to read him so well that she met his needs and he would never want to leave.

And she knew that was shit.

"Numb sounds dangerous," he said. "You're a bomb getting ready to go off and I don't know where to take cover from the fallout."

"If it'll relieve the suspense, I would like to kill you. I'd like to stone you publicly for adultery, although technically that's not true. I'd like to set fire to your study."

He raised his eyebrows.

"I'd like to tell the department chairman where you got that information for the article on Eliot."

"Now, wait a minute," he interrupted. "That was not illegal. My sources are perfectly legitimate." He had stopped pacing. "Besides, you promised." His voice rose.

"It may not be plagiarism, but it is suspect. And all bets are off, don't you think?" She was getting warmed up. "I could show Andrija the manuscript for your wonderful play and she would see just how much of it is in my handwriting. I wonder what that would do to her opinion of you?"

"You wouldn't."

"You don't know, do you, and that's what's on your mind. I could tell her how you behaved when your mother died and how I had to make the funeral arrangements. I barely knew the woman and she hated me because I wouldn't make you marry me."

Barb got up from the couch and stood directly in front of him on one of the Navahos.

"You just trashed me! You destroyed my life with no warning. You came back, married, fait accompli, to humiliate me in front of my friends and colleagues. I can't think of anything that would be too mean."

"You're being vindictive."

"Yes, and spiteful and petty and spleenful." She started pacing and he stood frozen, like a disgusting insect pinned to the board.

"I suppose I could sue you for something embarrassing and expensive," she said. "Get it in the papers. That would be fun."

"You'd get besmirched with the same mud."

"A little good, clean mudslinging would feel marvelous at this point. I could stomp you back, grind you into the muck. Andrija would rush to your defense, but the seeds of doubt would be planted. She'd hate me, but that's all right. I don't have anything to lose. I've already lost it."

The more she talked, the angrier she got.

"I could even tell her all the secret things we did in bed. Or your disgusting habits. I could parade all your inadequacies. You've certainly made me aware of all of mine."

"You castrating bitch!"

"I wish I were. I'd have them bronzed."

"If you think you could get by with that, you're sadly mistaken," he warned.

"O-ho. And what would you do?"

"Tell everybody how you keep your grades."

"Who cares?"

"Tell them you turn this house into a pigsty, can't keep the checkbook balanced."

"If you didn't like it, you could have taken care of that yourself."

"Frigid."

"Seems to me it was the opposite problem. You couldn't get it up. So I learned to not push it. I certainly didn't like being forced to beg."

"It's hard to get it up for a termagant."

"That's a good one. I'll have to look it up. Does it mean a woman who cleans up the vomit when you have the flu? The person who makes hot lemonade when your voice goes? The person who smiles and does nothing when your little-girl students ooze worship at your feet?"

"You got some of that yourself."

"Knowing how little there is in those pretty heads, knowing how utterly ignorant they are allows me to contain my lust."

"That sounds rehearsed."

"This isn't the first time I've said it," she snapped.

"So why did you stay if I was such a son of a bitch? What about all I did for you?"

"What?"

"It wasn't all one-sided, you know." He fidgeted beside the Morris chair.

"If you don't want to hear this, why did you come?" She circled him and the chair. "What did you expect? That I'd phone Hall's to see what pattern you registered and send you a butter knife? I know! You want me to play the shrew. Then you'll feel punished. Then you can go home to Andrija and marvel at the contrast." That cooled her off like a bucket of water over her head.

"We were good partners, once," he said. The low voice rumbled and reached her as it always had.

She stopped and grabbed the doorjamb. He wasn't playing fair. He remembered the good parts. She had to look away from him, and when she glanced down the hall, she could see the comforter folded over the end of the bed they had shared. The sight of their bed stopped her.

"Right," she said. And her voice was quiet again. "Seven good years, give or take a few months here and there. Stability. Security. Affection. Caring. Navaho rugs."

"You know it was more than that," he said. He moved toward her. "There was love and those were the good times."

"Yeah, you're right."

"I didn't set out to do this just to hurt you. It happened."

"And it can't unhappen."

"I'm sorry."

She reached out for him and he walked into a hug and they held each other for a long time.

"It was too sudden." She backed away and looked at him carefully. "It was unnecessarily cruel."

He nodded.

"It's going to take some time before I get used to not loving you, to your not loving me. In the meantime it hurts."

"I know. Guilty on all counts. I still care about you, I want you to know that. I did hurt you and I'm sorry I had to do that. I keep forgetting, too." He turned away and sank into the Morris chair. It had always been "his" chair. Maybe she could get him to take it.

"I'll read a line of poetry and think of you or I'll see something you'd enjoy and I start to think, I'll have to tell Barb about this, and then I remember that I can't."

"I know the feeling." She sat opposite him on the couch. "Little things, everyday things," she said. "I almost bought orange marmalade for you at the grocery store yesterday."

"I bought you silver pendants in Zagreb."

"Well, you'll have me crying in a minute and I won't have that."

They just stared at each other for a while, then she took a deep breath. "I won't do anything vengeful. I would like the house. I'm not going to sort through all the books to find yours."

"Set them aside as you run into them. It feels

liberating not to be surrounded by paper for a while."

"You can't stay in an apartment forever."

"When things settle down, we'll look for a house. Probably this summer."

"I think I'll go away this summer. I have leave time to work on that article and I have a new class to prepare for."

"Where will you go?"

She didn't answer. It was an automatic response. They were used to telling each other everything. Now it was none of his business. It felt lonely.

"I'll visit a friend out west. It'll give people a chance to get used to Andrija."

The last bit of energy drained. She knew the bad time wasn't over, but they had cleared the air. She was too tired to feel the anger and the sadness and the gray betrayal for a while.

They arranged to work out the details. She went to bed and slept fourteen hours, until daylight came.

9

The next night Barb went to the cabinet where she kept the liquor. Half a bottle of Red Label. Two inches of Canadian. Half a bottle of Spanish brandy. Liqueurs.

She carried the Scotch with her to the couch. It took a long time to drink it, a long time before she could sleep. The next morning she was sick—headache, nausea, the whole hangover. Driving the porcelain bus. She waited until the aspirin would stay down and went to work. She would not miss a day, no matter how bad she felt or what she did to herself.

The Valium was tempting. Nice muscle relaxant. Lets you sleep. No problems. But she knew that there would never be enough Valium in the world. Even if her doctor would prescribe it, which he wouldn't. There wasn't enough booze, or drugs, or anything else this side of a general anesthesia to make it quit hurting. If she could have stayed enraged all the time, maybe she could have handled it better. Maybe if she were religious, that would have helped, but she didn't expect sweet Jesus personally to come and warm her bed and tell her how to get through her days, how to forget what had happened.

As long as Barb concentrated, she was all right. Classes were fine and she read each student's end-of-term paper twice and wrote long comments. Her article on women's memoirs of the Santa Fe Trail grew. She upped her miles running in the morning and left her desk to work in the yard. Her roses and marigolds were weedless and perfect. She cleaned the house. Even did windows. Anything so she could quit staring at the night city sky through the branches of the late-leafing walnut tree outside the bedroom window and sleep.

She was muffled in an enormous half-filled gray balloon, a malfunctioning government weather balloon, struck by lightning during a storm. It settled over her and wouldn't go away. She pushed it away for a while, but when she stopped concentrating, it drooped over her, made it hard to breathe. She tried to punch holes in it, but the harder she worked, the more tangled she got. She went through those days like a windup toy, afraid to run down or relax because the balloon would smother her. As long as she kept moving, however mechanically, she didn't have to feel the Point-Seven Richter-scale earthquake that tumbled misery and self-loathing and insecurity around her. And ground her into the dirt because she knew absolutely that no one would ever love her again. That she never deserved to be loved.

There was a day when Grimaldi came over to fill boxes with clothes, papers, and books. He phoned first and was very polite. He cleared out his junk, cleaned up after himself. Barb couldn't work in the yard that rainy evening and puttered in the kitchen until ten. Then she went to the doorway of his study as he loaded folders into cardboard file drawers.

"I hope you count on a lot of time to get those papers organized," she said.

"What difference does it make to you?" he answered.

"You never could find anything."

"That's one thing I always loved about you," he said, huffing as he dragged an armload of folders to the box. "You always let me know how wonderful I am."

"Thanks." That hurt. "Just trying to make a constructive comment."

"Andrija thinks I'm okay just the way I am."

"You get unconditional acceptance from her."

"Which I never got from you."

"I reserve the right to call an asshole an asshole, especially when it affects me," she said.

"I never did anything right, by your standards."

"I spent seven years training you to be a human being with some thought for someone besides yourself. I had to teach you to wash clothes," she continued. "It's amazing. A man with a Ph.D. who can play chess and otherwise demonstrate his ability to function in the world can't learn how to dump in the dirty clothes and turn that little dial. It took you two years to learn where I kept the vacuum cleaner."

"I paid for half of everything," he said defensively.

"But you didn't do half of the scutwork. And all that time," she mocked, "I thought you loved me for my mind."

"And your body, of course," he said.

That hurt, but she'd asked for it. She thought back over seven years of loving Grimaldi, of putting up with his moods, of all the good times and the bitch-off times they had together. She supposed he thought of the time as "putting up with her moods" and wondered at the harsh treatment she handed him. His mother had certainly never obliged him to get groceries and—horrors!—fix his own meals.

"Why did you stay with me so long if you didn't like it?" she asked.

"I never found anybody better," he said. "Until Andrija."

Barb turned away and walked stiff-legged down the hall. She couldn't hide how bad that hurt. Major body blow. She couldn't breathe and felt dizzy and couldn't see, as though her blood pressure suddenly dropped. She sat on the edge of the bed and waited till vision returned, scared because her heart beat so fast. All along she'd thought they had a good thing going. They got along, had good times, had great sex, supported each other, took care of business. And all that time he would have left if he'd found somebody better. Better than what?

She ran her fingers through her thick hair and pulled until it hurt. She could make this pain stop. She choked back the sobs.

LOVE WITH A WARM COWBOY 83

♦ ♦ ♦

There was one party Barb couldn't avoid, a retirement party for Professor Reese at the home of the department chairman. The Sorensons came and picked her up.

She knew Andrija would be at the party and didn't want to go, but knew she'd have to face it sooner or later. She greeted people and worked her way to the drinks in the dining room. She glanced at the loaded buffet table and her nervous stomach cringed shut. She tried not to be obvious as she scanned for Grimaldi and Andrija.

It was a shining spring day and the party had spread out to the deck. She made her way through the rooms, chatting and trying to act normal. There was the animated chatter and the sound of ice in the glasses, voices raised in arch humor or murmuring with rosy gossip. The men wore light jackets or were in shirt sleeves and the women wore summer pastels. Then, as she sank onto one of the benches that edged the deck, she spotted them. Andrija stood poised and lovely in a flowered dress, one hand gracefully shading her big, dark eyes from the sun. Pre-Raphaelite hair curled around her face. There was something exotic—perhaps the uptilt of the eyes or the width of cheekbone. Grimaldi stood beside her, talking to Dr. Wilkins. He looked happy, like a man in love.

Barb's drink started shaking in her hand and she put it down before she spilled it. Then Grimaldi saw her and stopped. He said something to Andrija and they moved toward her. She stood up.

"Barb, I want you to meet Andrija."

Barb shook Andrija's hand briefly.

"Best wishes," Barb said, grateful for the formula. "I hope you'll be very happy."

"I'm glad to meet you," Andrija said. British accent, voice high and light.

And Barb had the goofy thought that if they had met in other circumstances, they would have been good friends.

"I understand that this has been a shock." Andrija's voice was sympathetic and Barb thought she meant it.

"Kind of you to realize." Barb was doing okay up till then. Stood up straight, smiled, voice steady. But she wasn't prepared for kindness. She gave Andrija a brief hug. Then she turned and walked back inside the house. Tears rolled down her face, but she knew wiping them was more noticeable than letting them run. She found the bathroom and waited until they stopped. She looked funny in the mirror, like some woman whose reflection she mistook for her own. She wished she had come in her own car; the Sorensons wouldn't be ready to leave yet. She was trapped without a car.

Dr. Wilkins just happened to be standing in the hall when she came out.

"Like a ride?" he asked.

"Yeah, I would." Her voice shook.

"You all right?"

"Silly to come to the party and leave so soon."

Barb held on to his arm and he led her out the door and drove her home.

◆ ◆ ◆

LOVE WITH A WARM COWBOY 85

Two days before "Grades Due" Grimaldi came over for the last of his things. Barb had found a few odds and ends—a handkerchief in with the sheets, a paperweight she used in the kitchen on cookbooks, a book on aerobics, an envelope with two tens tucked in a copy of *Old Possum's Book of Practical Cats*.

"Well, babe, this looks like the last of it," he said. He looked good and Barb hated that. She had dropped some weight.

"If I find anything else, I'll put it aside. What about the books?" she asked.

"Throw mine in a box and let me know when it's full, I guess."

She remembered the odd stuff and went to the kitchen, put the weight in a paper bag, and the book and the envelope and Eliot's cat poems. She held the handkerchief for a moment, looked at the frayed monogram, remembered the nosebleed that had stained it. Instead of putting it in the bag with the other detritus, she tucked it in the drawer with the dishtowels and took the bag out to him.

"You going to visit your friend?" he asked.

"I always visit Karen in the summer."

They looked at each other, both uncomfortable.

"Stay healthy," he said.

"Do good," she answered. And he left.

She wanted to warn Andrija: He's going to go tragic one of these days. All your love isn't going to keep him from plunging into depression. All the warmth and sensitivity that attracted you to him, all the vulnerable, boyish charm is going to disappear. The humor will vanish. You'll spend months with someone who's thinking how wretched the world is, who ponders future calamities.

And what scared her was, he wouldn't. That Andrija was what he had needed all along. That she was the magic something that would keep him from depression, who really would make him happy forever.

And if she did?

Then this is the right thing for Grimaldi and she wasn't.

Then seven years was a mistake. For both of them.

With his office emptied, there was no reason to treat it as sacrosanct. It was just another room in the house. Her house. One Saturday morning when rain sheeted down, flattening the irises and shattering the tulip petals in the yard, she took a bucket and rags into the office. Clean places stood out from the year's dust, where he'd removed papers and books. She started with the cobwebs at the ceiling and worked her way down. Scrubbed the walls, oiled the paneling, used wood cleaner on shelves. She took down the curtains to go to the cleaners and dusted the blinds with a pair of old cotton gloves, did the windows, took a brush to the baseboards. She dragged the odd table to the basement, wheeled the swivel chair into the hallway, and started on the desk. He would claim it, she knew, because it was monumental, fitting his image of himself. She cleaned the top, then dumped the odd paper clip and corner dust from the drawers into a trash bag. There were some papers and junk in the bottom drawer he hadn't wanted. When she tipped them out, she saw snapshots.

She aligned them on the desktop. He had left pictures of them. Her at the lake, looking silly in cutoffs, with a beer in each hand. Him in Taos, his cowboy hat so new it glistened. Them together, at the cathedral in Santa Fe, a photo taken by an obliging fellow tourist. Hot tears burned. He didn't even care enough to keep a few snapshots. Not even of himself. The picture she'd taken of him beaming beside his new car. A shot from a party where he'd been talking and didn't know she was focused on him.

I'm not going to cry, Barb thought. I'm mad as hell. Where did he get off leaving these behind? Did he think he could forget seven years if he didn't have these to remind him?

She ripped the snapshots apart into neat quarters, but that didn't feel good enough, so she twisted and tore, obliterating them. She was crying and hiccuping. Tears blinded her. She rocked, hugged herself to keep from coming apart.

When she could get up, she shoved the drawers back in the desk, gave it a lick and a promise. It took the last dredges of energy to push the chair back into the room and slam the door behind her.

10

"Grades Due" day came. Barb pulled into her parking space in her repaired station wagon. It had taken three years to get from the phys.-ed. lot six blocks away to a lot next to the building where her office was. It took ten minutes at a faculty meeting to get a parking space she had been entitled to all along. Dr. Wilkins said the infighting in academe was the most bitter in the world because so little was at stake.

It was a lovely spring day. Oaks and elms arched over the walks. Flowers bloomed in their cedar-chip beds. Birds sang. Teenage lovers strolled hand in hand, hormones pumping. Crusty professors doddered, clutching sere and yellowed notes they hadn't revised in twenty years. They smiled benevolently as they began a summer of the grant-supported estivation they called research.

It all was gray for Barb.

She carried boxes of notes, Xeroxes, and books

for the article on Kate Chopin from her office to the car, then turned in her grades and said good-bye to the department chairman. Smile, joke, and hold herself together just a little while longer.

She had kept a stiff upper lip so long she thought it would crack. One more hour and her central nervous system would overload. She had gone through her Valium (for all the good it did) and was sleeping nights thanks only to Benadryl. Each day she realized more things that wouldn't be the same. Usually it was something little—she always took care of the cars and he dealt with plumbers.

After she turned grades in, she stocked up on frozen entrées, bought produce and dairy, and went home. She turned on the sprinkler for the front yard, changed into jeans and a sweatshirt. Then she lay on the couch and let the gray balloon sink over her. She didn't go to pieces; the pieces settled in on her. She was Not Feeling. She couldn't move because it took too much energy. She had gotten through the three weeks. Now what? She couldn't make any plans because her brain had clicked off. She got up every three or four hours and ate something and moved the sprinkler. It had been a dry spring.

After three days she quit moving the sprinkler. She quit getting up to change tapes. Even Mozart didn't help. The books on the end table gathered dust. When her neighbor hadn't seen Barb for several days, she came by.

"I thought you might be sick and need something," said the elderly woman. "You do look pale." Her motherly face showed her concern. Barb had told her about Grimaldi.

"No, I'm fine for groceries. Just a touch of the flu. Thanks." Rejection flu. The dumped-on, kicked-over, crying-my-eyes-out blues.

Barb's mother phoned.

"I haven't heard from you, Barbara. Did your young man come back from Bulgaria?"

"Yugoslavia." Mom didn't know how to refer to Grimaldi, so he had become her young man.

"He came back married," Barb said.

"You got married!"

"No, Mom. He got married."

"To someone else?"

Barb heard the BarcaLounger creak as her mother sat up. She could picture the beautiful old face in tissue crepe wrinkles of puzzlement, uncomprehending.

"Yes, Mom. Brought back a Croatian bride. She's very nice."

"That's terrible. You don't sound right."

"I'm a little blue, Mom. Understandable."

"You should have made him marry you. He couldn't get out of it so easily if you were married."

"Right, Mom."

"Now, don't go feeling sorry for yourself. Good riddance to bad rubbish." Mom had a saying for every occasion. "It's an ill wind, you know."

"I'm keeping the house."

"There, you see?" After a pause she said, "Do you need anything, dear. I hate to think of your rattling around alone in that empty house. Would you like for me to stay with you for a while?"

"I've been alone since last August."

"Well, I just don't want you to feel bad. I mean you probably felt bad at first, but you can find a real husband now."

"I don't think I'll start looking just yet."

"Of course, dear."

"How're Cindy and the kids?" Barb got a fifteen-minute update on soccer practice and swim meets and aerobics class and Sid, who was (lower your voice) Jewish, but the best husband in the world.

Barb had given up trying to be what her mother expected. She had made herself up as she went along, with Grimaldi. She needed to work out who she was without him.

Then Karen called on Memorial Day Monday.

"When are you coming?" she asked.

"I . . . well, it's been a rough semester and I thought I'd just rest here," Barb said. The thought of packing a bag overwhelmed her.

"What happened?" Barb could almost see the question in Karen's green eyes. There was a long silence on the line. Barb could hear scraps of words, of other people's lives. She could see Karen's porcelain cheeks and the fine blond hair around her face.

"Marty got married."

"I thought he was in Yugoslavia."

"That's where he got married."

"You mean that slimy bastard got married without telling you? What are you doing?"

"We're working out the legal details," Barb said.

"That's not what I meant."

"I'm lying on the couch. It's very restful."

"You sound funny. Like you're spaced out."

"No, just tired."

"I thought you were coming out to Cloud Peaks. Now you can stay the whole summer."

Barb couldn't tell Karen, whom she loved, that she couldn't make the effort, that she barely had the energy to talk. "No, I think I'll just stay here."

"Are you working on your article?"

"Yes, sure." Barb hadn't even unloaded the boxes from the car.

"Where's Grimaldi?"

"In an apartment on Wornall. In conjugal bliss, I assume."

"And you're lying on the couch?"

"That's about right."

"Are you going to stay there all summer?"

"I think so."

Karen was silent and Barb heard static on the line.

"We opened Cloud Peaks this weekend, to get things ready. I expect you by Friday."

"I really can't—"

"Yes, you can. If you don't show up, I'm coming to get you. Have you started packing?"

"No, I really—" The vegetables had gone slimy in the bottom of the fridge. Barb either needed to get the lawn mowed or declare it a Tallgrass Prairie Preservation area. She hadn't changed clothes or showered in two days.

"Listen to me!" Karen demanded. "I know you feel like shit. You ought to feel bad when bad things happen. But you're not staying there alone. Get a pen and paper."

Barb started to protest, but did as Karen ordered.

"Get the car checked, oil changed, and gassed up. Stop the paper, leave a forwarding address with the post office. Are you writing this down?"

"Yes." And she was.

"Do you have Marty's new phone number?"

"Right here, under Scuzzbucket."

"Give it to me. I'll tell him to take care of the yard."

"I don't want to go anywhere."

"That has nothing to do with it. Get your suitcases out and wash clothes and start packing. Bring boots and a warm coat."

"Yes, but it was ninety degrees here today. What do I need with a parka?"

"It gets cold in the mountains, even in the summer. Unless you find a warm cowboy. It snows in August up here."

"You're going to granny me until I get there, aren't you?"

"Damn right."

"Okay, okay."

"You're a mess now, but you'll be fine without Grimaldi once you pull yourself together."

Barb had to smile.

"When are you leaving Kansas City?" Karen asked.

"This is Monday, everything's closed. Tuesday to get packed and run errands. Wednesday morning, I guess."

"One night or two?"

"Probably two."

"Wednesday night, Thursday night, so Friday is about right. Call me before you leave."

"Right, Commander."

Karen giggled. Barb let herself be bossed because she knew Karen was doing it out of love, for her own good. She'd put up with it from Karen. "I need to get away." Once she said it, it sounded right. She wanted very much to be out of the situation, to escape the daily reminders of what had happened, to escape the strain of not letting the hurt show.

"I'll phone you Wednesday morning before I hit the road."

Barb hung up and looked around. With Karen's voice in her ear she set to work. She cleaned the fridge and gave what was salvageable to the neighbor and left her the key. She phoned Mom and gave her Karen's summer number. She packed, digging her parka from the back of the hall closet. Tuesday she ran errands, checked off the items on Karen's list, phoned to see if the guest-ranch wiring would take the computer. Karen said no, besides the generator went down from time to time.

Barb left the Kate Chopin notes where they were in the hatch, threw Marty's Taos hat in the trash, and loaded up the car. Then she drove to the interstate, found the hundred-eighty-degree look, and headed Elsewhere.

"So that's the story," said Barb.

Karen looked thoughtful, but not pitying. "That was a bitch. A gold-plated crock."

Barb nodded and blew her nose. She had cried, but kept going. She was glad she'd gotten through it. The yammer in her head had stopped, and the monologues with Marty. She didn't know what she was doing with Hal, only that she wanted to make love with him again.

"Well, I can see why you want to go with Hal," said Karen, "but I think it's a mistake. What're you getting out of it?"

"The best sex I ever had in my life."

Karen shrugged. "That's hard to argue with."

This time when Barb dialed, Hal answered. Her breath stopped in her throat.

"How was Hampton's?" she asked. Her mouth was so dry her teeth stuck to the inside of her lip.

"Fine. How's Cloud Peaks?" His voice was always lighter than she expected.

"Fine."

"How's everything?" he asked.

"Great," she said. What bright repartee. Silence on the line. "I'll tell you what I'm really thinking, if you will."

He laughed. "It's a deal."

"I really want to make love with you again."

Silence.

"You don't mince your words, do you?" he said.

"Too pushy?"

"Yes, but I'm getting used to it." He laughed again. "I was going to say something like that, too."

"That's a relief. I thought maybe you did this all the time and once more didn't mean anything."

"No, it meant something. Not sure what yet."

"Me neither."

"Well, uh, I guess I want to know when we can get together again." He sounded diffident and she wished she could slip through the phone lines into his arms.

"Do they have polo games every Sunday?" she asked.

"Almost. How about sooner than that?"

"Great. When and where are you working?"

"That's the problem." He sounded uncomfortable. Barb imagined him sitting at the heaped-over desk in the office in his trailer, looking at a calendar. "I've got to be in Gillette Friday night."

"What about Thursday night, tomorrow?" Did she sound too eager? So what.

"I could drive up when I finish. I'm shoeing for a ranch near Buffalo."

"I could drive down to Story."

"I might not get through when I expect to. You'd have to wait."

"I could read a good book."

She thought of the book-lined walls and the huge television set. They decided that she would drive down after dinner at Cloud Peaks. He didn't lock his trailer, so she could just go in and wait.

Then he said, "Now I wish I hadn't scheduled anything for tomorrow. I'll be thinking about you all day."

She felt light and happy. She was afraid she'd gone overboard and it was all one-sided.

"It's good to know you want this, too," she said.

"You bet I do."

11

Barb got to Hal's trailer about eight. The sun hadn't set, but the tall foothill trees brought early twilight to the little town. The mountains rose straight up behind the tall firs, and the foothills stretched gently downhill, log homes barely noticeable in the woods.

A tub of watered petunias and marigolds sat beside the porch steps, their blues and golds brilliant and vivid in the clear, high sun. A tiny creek sang beneath the aspens and chokecherry bushes behind the trailer. High up in the trees birds called. There was a light on inside, but Hal wasn't home. Barb had worked herself into an anxiety state. She had dressed carefully—clean jeans, pretty shirt, not too much makeup, hair fresh. Dinner rumbled unhappily in her belly. All her adolescent insecurities whispered, just out of earshot. All her middle-aged insecurities were operating, too. He'd think she was too old, too wrinkled. Not lubricious enough, not acrobatic enough. She almost got back in her car and left.

Stop that, she ordered herself. He wasn't perfect, either. She enjoyed his company, his conversation. This wasn't a beauty contest. People liked people in spite of, not because of. She and Hal had managed to get together in spite of differences. In spite of her not knowing anything about horses. In spite of his not looking like the Marlboro man or sounding like Grimaldi.

She liked him for his eyes that changed colors and his humor and his patience. And his rough hands and heavy shoulders.

Maybe that was enough.

She calmed down, stretched out on his couch. It was long and comfortable, sort of shabby, like hers, and the books made her feel at home. The last ocher rays of the sun threw rosy light through the windows. She did muscle-group relaxation and deep breathing and concentrated on the light and the sound of the trickling creek.

She woke up when he closed the door. It took a moment to remember where she was and she lay there blinking. He dropped a handful of ropes and stomped over to the couch in his boots. He leaned down and she raised up and they kissed. He smelled sweaty and horsey and felt wonderful. She pulled him down on top of her and wrapped her arms around him.

"I need to clean up, Barb," he managed, when they broke for air.

"Mmm," she said. She held his face in her hands. She could feel the bloom of his skin and the scratch of his whiskers, the moisture of his breath, and the taste of his mouth. She squirmed out of her shirt and bra as he pushed his Levi's down, then sat to pull off his boots. He tugged her jeans off and knelt beside the couch.

"Hi, honey, I'm home."

She laughed.

"Are you always this ready?" he asked. It wasn't a serious question. He rested his hand on her stomach and spread his rough, scarred fingers. She groaned.

"You like that, huh?"

"I like everything." The warmth of his hand comforted and excited. She reached to draw him into her arms, but he slid down the length of her body.

"What are you doing?"

"Mmmm, mmmm."

"I can't stop I can't stop I can't stop." She grabbed the arm of the couch because she was flying off into space.

When she opened her eyes, she saw him looking down at her. "You're watching me make faces." She was breathless.

"I'm enjoying watching you."

"Join me," she gasped.

He eased onto the couch and braced himself. She felt him, but not his weight. "You're watching again," she whispered.

"You're incredible," he said, and shifted to free one hand.

"Wonderful," she managed.

◆ ◆ ◆

"Did you have any dinner?" she asked afterward, measuring canned Colombian into a Mr. Coffee basket.

"Earlier."

"Good, I ate, too. I'm not much of a cook." She shoved the basket into the machine.

They sat together in affectionate silence.

"No conversation?" he said in a teasing tone.

"I'm enjoying the moment."

"You're only interested in one thing," he said, and she burst out laughing.

"I am." She wondered what he was interested in. Tony hadn't meant much—balm to her ego, soothing to her flesh. There were all kinds of variations to the game. She wondered what Hal was thinking. She said, "I've never been carried away like this, never allowed myself to be. Didn't know I could do these things."

"Don't analyze it." He seemed to be wondering what it all meant, too.

"Where do you come from?" she asked. "What made you this way? Why do you like me? My hair is straight, my teeth are crooked, and my ass is too big."

"You smell good, your hair is soft, and when I grab your ass I know I've got hold of something."

"Tell me who you are."

"I grew up on a ranch just over the Montana line. I went to school, worked on another ranch."

"With horses?"

"Usually, but hands do what there is to do—move cattle, put up hay, whatever."

"How did you start as a farrier?"

"Went to school, bought the equipment. That was two years ago."

"Why didn't you stay in Montana?"

"More horses around here." He looked at her and smoothed her hair. "I know you teach college in Kansas City. How did you get here?"

"I guess it's only fair to tell you." I took a deep breath and gave him the Cliff's Notes summary of Grimaldi's Betrayal. She didn't cry much.

He gave a low whistle when she finished.

"Right. So I came here to put myself together, find out how to be single again."

"After a couple of years you'll be able to talk about it, but you won't," Hal said.

"Did something like that happen to you?"

"I was married. We've been separated . . . it'll be three years ago September."

"Bad?"

"I thought so."

"I wonder if that's why we hit it off—we had this in common." It was getting intense, so Barb got up and poured coffee for them. "Read any good books lately?" she asked. She heard him take a big breath and his eyes came back from where they had been, remembering.

"Well, last week I read *The Mind's Eye*, about ways of looking at consciousness," he said.

"I saw it in the bookstore. I thought it would be all computers," she said.

"Same guy wrote *Gödel, Escher, Bach*."

"Then you're way ahead of me because I couldn't get through that one."

He looked at her, disbelieving.

"I know what I know," she said, a little defensive. "That's American literature and how to write academic stuff and a few other things. But I don't know any physics or anything about computers except how to work my word processor. Or about horses. Or how my car works. I don't even know how people work, what makes them tick."

"You don't have to play dumb for me," said Hal. He sounded angry. She turned and he looked angry.

"I'm not playing," she said. "I see how you live and how you fit into your environment. I live a precious and artificial life, made up of books and papers and marks on your record. Most of the time I feel okay and think I'm hot poop. Here in Wyoming, I'm out of my element. I feel how much I lack. And how much I've missed."

"Don't patronize me," he said, still wary.

"I'll patronize you," she said, and put her coffee cup down. She took his and put it on the table. "I'll simonize you and categorize you and vulcanize you." She poked him in the chest with each threat. "I'll analyze you and synthesize you." This time he went back and she was on top. "I'll elegize you and computerize you and anthologize you."

Somewhere in the list she got distracted and the coffee went cold in the cups.

They did talk, later, those exchanges of information that begin a friendship. They didn't sleep much and it was a good thing he didn't have to be in Gillette first thing in the morning. Barb felt no compulsion to race back up the mountain and go to work on the article. They arranged to meet in Sheridan Saturday afternoon. He would help her buy a hat, they'd have dinner and a few drinks.

LOVE WITH A WARM COWBOY 103

♦ ♦ ♦

That Saturday she drove into town, not feeling completely confident. She expected to be left waiting at the Custom Cowboy, pretending she was interested in halters and bits and saddles. They'd never pledged undying love. She had nothing she could count on and it made her jumpy.

Hal arrived at the appointed time and she started breathing. She couldn't get this tense every time she arranged to meet a man. If she didn't get over it, she'd quit trying.

"We've got to find you a hat," he said.

"I brought money."

"Now, a really good hat costs a little money, but a hand wears it in the sun and rain every day. So it's really an investment."

"I just need something for when I'm out of the car."

He pondered as he looked down the row of hats displayed above the tack, which covered one wall. Custom Cowboy smelled of good leather and dry goods. They made and repaired saddles, and one battered example lay beside an industrial sewing machine and another sat on a stand on the tan tile floor. Strips and scraps of leather littered the worktables. Prices for new saddles were astounding—fifteen hundred dollars and more. The prices for hats seemed high, too, seventy dollars for nothing special. They had good prices for nifty split-back dusters and jean jackets and rawhide gloves and Cattle Kate reproduction period dresses. She'd come back later for them.

Hal started with a high-crowned, big-brimmed

hat suitable for Hoss Cartwright and worked his way down the row of displayed hats.

"Why the face?" he asked as she tried one on.

"I feel like an idiot."

"You look fine." He stood just behind her and she could see both of them in the etched mirror in the dark oak frame. He looked calm and happy. His good hat belonged on his head. His short hair barely showed. He smiled and she could tell he was enjoying himself. She frowned as she turned from side to side. The hat didn't look right. Her hair hung straight beneath the brim, which shadowed her face. The pinch marks under the cheekbones were fading, but her mouth was a thin-lipped, downturned slash.

Hal pushed a crease into the crown and adjusted it so that the brim tilted ten degrees down.

"It makes me look as though I were pretending to be something I'm not. A native," she said.

"You want to look like a tourist?"

"Not really. But a hat doesn't make a hand."

"We don't have to do this," he said very quietly.

"You were kind enough to offer to help me buy a hat so my nose could quit peeling."

"But you don't have to take me up on it." He had a faint air of someone trying to reason with a four-year-old.

"I guess I'm being silly. People out here put great importance on hats. The hats separate the natives from the dudes. I'm going to look like a dude anyway, it'll be so new."

"Let's forget about it."

"No. Let's take it."

She gave the hat to the clerk to be blocked in a

buckaroo crease. Buying the damned hat, a serviceable brown, seemed to be fraught with some kind of significance, but she couldn't identify it. If I buy a real cowboy hat, she wondered, does that say, "I want to be here. I want to be one of you?" She was afraid she'd look ridiculous. It felt like the first step toward something. Being with Hal felt good, but she didn't want to lose herself.

She paid for the hat and pushed it carefully on her head. They walked outside, hadn't taken two steps when the wind lifted the hat off and sent it down Main Street. Hal and Barb ran for it. She caught it and pushed it down hard before the wind took it again, and she wondered if she would spend the summer holding her hat in place.

"You need a stampede string," Hal said.

"I'd have to punch holes in my new hat."

"I wonder why girls have trouble keeping their hats on. Maybe it's all that hair." He smoothed the hair at her shoulder with the back of his hand. He touched her peeling nose with one rough finger. "I'll miss your sunburn."

"Let's do it," she said. They went back into the store and the clerk punched holes, put in grommets, and threaded a rawhide string through the holes. He pushed the ends through a wooden bead and they left again. This time Barb tightened the string when the sun-bright wind tried to blow the hat away. The brim and sunglasses shaded her eyes and immediately she felt the relief.

The sun shone brighter in Sheridan. The air was so clear you could see the peaks and the canyon cuts of the Big Horns. No humidity blurred the edges, no smog darkened the colors. The sky was bigger and higher and bluer. It was four thousand feet—not so high the altitude zapped her, but high enough to be cool and closer to the sun.

They drove down Sheridan's main street, where she saw old buildings and men in jeans and hats walking bowlegged in their boots and she could imagine how it looked in the old days. There were stores selling ropes and camping gear and western clothes, as well as the usual kinds of things. The hill where the rest of Sheridan lived rose on their left as they headed to the Golden Steer.

It was appropriate to eat at a steakhouse in this beef-raising country. The dim room was maroon-carpeted and comfortable, the service prompt and unintrusive. Good steakhouses have their own atmosphere, as though the walls and tables and chairs have absorbed the satisfaction of patrons well fed. They ordered drinks and nibbled out of the relish tray.

"Why did you hesitate over the hat, Barb?" Hal asked. He wore a long-sleeved plaid shirt and clean, pressed jeans. His short hair and mustache were trimmed. He looked at home in the world and the men at the other tables in three-piece suits or Bermuda shorts looked absurd. This was Wyoming—comfortable and laid-back. Denim and cotton, big belt buckles, boots, and hats. What would look ridiculous in Milwaukee or New Jersey or Kansas City looked just right out here.

"I don't know," she said. "I don't like to shop, Hal. I go to a store, buy what I need, and leave."

"You weren't born to shop?"

"What kind of thing is that to say? Because I'm a

brown, sage-dotted hills and the creeks that raced down from the reservoirs.

"When do you go back?" he asked.

"The end of August, in time for the semester."

She didn't like thinking about that. He looked morose and said nothing. What was going to happen? They had a few weeks. If they got serious, it would be harder to say good-bye. They didn't hold back in bed. Sometimes when Barb had made love with Grimaldi, she had the feeling his mind was somewhere else and he was phoning it in. Maybe that's the way it always gets if enough time passes. When Hal looked at her with his blue eyes that soaked up the color of the sky or the grass or the air, he was one hundred percent there. It was the teasing, the gentle touches. It was laughing in the right places. Most of all, when she looked in his eyes, she knew all his attention focused on what they were doing. She didn't have to fight a fog of depression to reach him.

They both had a lot of armor still in place, things they hadn't told about themselves.

"That's the first I've thought about leaving and it already makes me sad," Barb said.

She expected him to say something comforting, but he just looked at her and now his eyes were dark in the dim light of the restaurant and she couldn't read them.

She felt restless and uncomfortable and it was easy to start a fight when they went to the Mint Bar after dinner.

12

Barb and Hal got bottled Budweiser and worked their way past the tourists and locals to a booth in the back room. The booths were wood, bent and curved and stained a dark brown, with cushioned seats. It was early and the bar wasn't crowded. Hal said hello to several people, including an older man nursing a highball.

"A customer?" Barb asked.

"Owned a big ranch until a couple of years ago. Had to take chapter eleven, I think it was. Get reorganized. His brothers and sisters back east made him hire a manager. He's still got enough money left to trade a few horses."

Barb printed wet rings from the bottom of the bottle in overlapping circles on the battered, varnished tabletop. "What's going to happen to us?"

"We're going to enjoy each other and have a good time."

"At the end of the summer?"

"It's too early to think about that. Anything could happen. We could both be dead. Never anticipate, never expect anything. Then you don't get disappointed."

"I feel like you just slapped my hands as I reached for a cookie." She had been reaching for something that was an illusion at best and deceptive always. She felt rotten. She couldn't just be there, couldn't just enjoy the evening. She still wanted reassurance and knew there would never be enough.

He reached across the table and squeezed her hand. She felt like pulling away. She could smell his Old Spice.

"Don't be so prickly," he said.

"You've been so nice I haven't had an excuse to be bitchy, but tonight I got the feeling that I'm not half as smart as I think I am and that rubs."

"You're smart. You're pretty. You're fabulous. You've got one of the all-time great asses. Your eyes cross when you orgasm. Is that enough?"

"I guess it has to be. I wish you'd do something gross and I could get mad. If I was mad, I wouldn't be thinking about having to leave Wyoming."

"Fine, what do you want to fight about?" Hal made sparring movements with his big hands.

"Like, why you kept your degree a secret. You knew it would make an impression on me. You saved that little bit of information to unbalance me."

"You're right, I did." He grinned and Barb knew that tack wasn't going to work.

"And your little girl." She didn't know what to think about that.

He shrugged.

"You never thought of birth control," she said.

"I like babies."

"That's bullshit."

"Out here people do what they want to do and take responsibility for it," he said. "You want to drink and drive? Then you've got to take the DUIs. You don't want a baby, take care of it."

"Do you plan to take care of it?" She'd refilled her prescription for birth-control pills in May, anticipating Grimaldi's return.

"Don't you use something?" he asked.

"As a matter of fact, no." She watched his mouth drop open. "I like babies, too."

"You're teasing."

"You don't know. You never gave it a thought. If there was a baby, it would be my problem, wouldn't it?"

Women in romance novels never have cramps or periods, thought Barb. Never get pregnant unless it's necessary to the plot. Well, she wasn't living on a pink cover in a swirling décolleté gown, a darkly handsome man in a billowing white shirt embracing her protectively. When they were popular she tried to read romances, thinking she could write one, but she kept wanting to throw up. The heroine always had to choose between a safe, boring man and an exciting, unsuitable man. Usually the exciting unsuitable man practically raped the heroine at some point. That way she didn't have to be morally responsible, even if she wanted it. She got carried away. And nobody mentioned PMS.

LOVE WITH A WARM COWBOY 113

Hal was silent. Frowned. Cleared his throat. "Would you like me to get some condoms?"

"That's usually the simplest way."

"If you don't do anything, you were taking a hell of a chance," he mused. He was unbelieving. "Not even the pill?"

"Why should I take a drug that has dangerous side effects when my former lover was out of the country for ten months?"

"Weren't you afraid you'd get pregnant when we made love?"

"Yeah, well, I wasn't thinking. Overcome by lust." Barb smiled. "Yes, I use something. Don't worry."

He looked relieved.

Something about buying the hat was wrong and she couldn't figure out why it made her uncomfortable. She felt she was spinning out of control and didn't know why and didn't know how to stop it. She was churning up bitterness and getting disgusted. She couldn't face things ending. She never could stand to pull adhesive tape off slowly.

She got up and walked to the front of the bar, bought another round, and walked to the booth. She knew she was acting awful. But she felt bad and unsettled, wanted to scream ugly names. If she really got involved with Hal, she'd care about him, and somewhere down the road, in a month or two, she'd be hurting.

She picked up her purse and walked out the front door without looking at Hal or saying anything. Without knowing why she did it. She walked to her car and drove to the Good Times

Bar, where there was a loud band and dancing. She left her new hat at the Mint Bar.

A blast of music from the three-piece combo reached her from the small platform at the back of the room. Couples crowded the dance floor, swinging each other to the drummer's steady beat. Barb bought herself a beer and watched, waiting to cool off, wishing she knew what the hell she was doing. Well, she would drink and listen to the music and study the elk heads and the dancers and after a while she'd drive back to Cloud Peaks. She would *not think* about Hal.

Barb told Karen she wanted something fast and simple, but it was getting serious and intense. Or maybe it was just Barb. She wasn't ready to give up the protective armor that kept her from getting close to someone. Under the armor was a pale, soft center.

She saw a couple of people she had met at the Outlaws and joined a group of men and girls at the bar who were listening to Curry Cannon whom Barb had met at the Outlaws.

Curry was crisply turned out in a laundry-creased shirt, spotless jeans, and a summer straw Stetson that looked riveted in place. Maybe it was the hat, pulled down to half an inch above his eyebrows, that gave him a dim look. Then it registered and Barb almost dropped her beer. This was Jim Bob. She knew Curry worked on a ranch east of Ucross, came into town on weekends, like a soldier on leave. He had that all-weather tan and muscles straining the plaid shirt and eyes as blue and pale as the Douglas carwash cowboy.

"This cop stopped me," Curry said. "I was driving in this park in Denver. And when he looked in the pickup, there was this woman giving me a blow job."

People around Curry laughed. Barb usually ignored stories like that, but she kept listening. And *not thinking*.

"She never even stopped till we were done. And the cop said, 'I don't know what to write on the ticket.' Hell, I didn't know what to say. I must have been driving funny. It was a miracle I kept the pickup on the road. Then the cop said, 'I'm going to put down obstructing the view of the driver.' So I said, 'Sounds okay to me.'"

Everybody laughed. He was feeling his Coors tonight and he had an audience.

"It cost me thirty-eight hundred dollars to get my shoulder fixed," he said, "so I never did get my wrist taken care of. But except for that I was good at rodeoing." His listeners laughed and one reminded him of all the falls he had taken bull riding.

"Yeah," continued Curry. "But that wasn't how I got hurt. I'm acrobatic. I knew how to fall."

"Then why did you quit?" asked a blond girl.

"Got tired of bull snot in my back pocket," said Curry.

"What?" Barb asked.

"Bull snot. Dropping down on my backside when I was on the ground."

"What else did you do, rodeoing?" she asked.

"Roping, bronc riding, all that stuff."

"Why'd you quit?" Barb studied his bland face. He was so damned clean-cut. Blue eyes, pink cheeks, close shave, trimmed hair, hard body. He looked like all the B-western extras of her childhood.

"Well, I got into trouble with that old sumbitch I was working for, at Arvada. It wasn't nothing. I didn't go to do it on purpose, but he got mean and called the cops on me."

"What'd you do?"

"I set his foreman's house on fire."

"Just like that?"

"Well, I was using this propane branding iron and I got too close to the siding, and the next thing I knew, the house was on fire."

"Sounds like you're—"

"Accident prone, that's what they say. Anyway, I had a choice and I went in the army instead of jail and that was the end of rodeoing for me."

"What do you do now?"

"Whatever the boss tells me—fix fences, move cattle, put up hay, take care of the horses, shoe them. In the spring there's calving, and we just finished branding."

"Sounds interesting," she said.

"Not as interesting as being here. Would you like to dance?"

"I'm not sure I can. If you don't mind getting your feet stepped on."

Curry placed a hand lightly on Barb's back and they walked onto the dance floor. The combo was doing a slow, non–Willie Nelson version of "Whiskey River" and Curry swung her in front of him and wrapped an arm around her waist and took her hand and gently started the steps. It wasn't very complicated, but when she tried to think of what she should be doing, she stumbled and lost the beat. She would *not think* about Hal or feeling bad or anything. She would dance and drink enough to feel the edges soften and listen to Curry bullshit about his accidents.

She laughed, mostly from nervousness, and he just kept steering her back and forth. He sang along with the band, and surprisingly he was on key. In fact, it sounded kind of nice to have his voice soft in her ear, his cheek on hers. Occasionally she knocked his hat loose, but he'd calmly screw it back in place.

The band went into a fast version of "Honky-tonk Man" and Barb tried to keep up with Curry. For a beefy guy, he was light on his feet and danced tirelessly. Her awkwardness didn't seem to bother him and he patiently got her back on the beat until she was more or less following him. His hand slipped down her back to her waist, then to her ass, and at first she didn't even notice. It felt normal to have a hand there. Then she remembered she had just met him and pulled it back up.

After half a dozen dances the band took a break and Curry led Barb to a table and bought her a beer. She asked him about his work and he told her and joked. She asked him a few things about shoeing she hadn't asked Hal, but all she got were one-sentence answers. He didn't shoe full-time like Hal, maybe because of his reputation for "accidents."

"I think I can tell the real cowboys from the tourists by now," Barb said. "Now, there's a real cowboy." She indicated a man in a checked wool shirt over a red long-john top, twill pants, and lace-up work boots.

"Naw, that's a buckaroo," said Curry. "He's from California and manages the computer store. People like that dress up trying to look like natives." His voice was full of scorn.

"I guess he does look a little studied. Like he's in the road company of *Paint Your Wagon*. But it's easy to tell the tourists."

"If they're wearing shorts, they're tourists."

"Don't natives wear shorts?"

"Not when they go out."

"But they don't always dress western." She thought of Hal's knit shirts.

"Naw, they wear whatever they want."

"Can you tell I'm not a native?"

"Sure."

She waited. "Well, what makes me different?"

"It's hard to say. Maybe you just look different. Some women come out here and buy western clothes and everything's so new, you know they're tourists."

She wasn't wearing anything new, so she waited for Curry to explain, but he wasn't up to analyzing the dude look.

They danced again and she felt a little drunk. It was easy to lean against Curry and let him lead her around the floor. He did a lot of "sugar, honey, baby, sweetie" stuff, told her she had a great body. He sang some more, his mouth close to her ear. After a while he stopped singing and started kissing and nuzzling her neck. She pulled away, but in a few minutes he was back again and it seemed like too much trouble to stop him. His hand slipped down to her ass more often and she let it stay. It was pleasantly mindless to sway and shuffle and *not think* about anything in particular.

After another round of beer and dancing, he asked, "Would you like to go home with me?"

"Where's home?" she asked. She had trouble concentrating.

"I got this little house outside Sheridan," he said. "Well, it's not mine, but my uncle is off on a pack trip over by Jackson and I stay there on weekends."

"What would we do at your uncle's?" She knew damned well what they'd do, but she wanted to hear what he'd say.

"Well, we could put a pizza in the microwave and turn on the late movie and then we'll see what we could do."

For some reason that sounded appealing. She wouldn't be able to think about Hal if she went. She wouldn't have to think at all. Curry was Jim Bob. No Coors belt buckle, but all the other qualifications. Hadn't she said she wanted uncomplicated sex, a warm cowboy? Here he was—John Wayne and apple pie and the American flag. She could fuck the archetype, the dude lady's dream. She tried to think of reasons why she shouldn't go home with Curry, but she was foggy from beer. And she didn't want to talk herself out of it. She wondered if there was a gun rack in his pickup.

She left her car in the Good Times parking lot and got in Curry's truck. The floor was littered with rust-red gravel, fast-food containers, and empty beer cans. A brown plaid bath towel covered the shredded upholstery. Curry said his dog tore it up. Barb looked for the seat belt, but it had disappeared and she wasn't in the mood to dig for it. She felt hazy and was riding without a safety belt anyway.

He drove south on Main and turned off the highway at the edge of the city. They bounced down a long gravel drive and around some trees to a small frame house with a dog tied to the front porch. The dog, a sheepdog mix, went berserk, barking and leaping against the rope. Barb didn't know if he was any good scaring away burglars, but he convinced her. Curry hollered, "Shut up, Igor," on his way past and the dog subsided.

Well, a dog named Bubba was too much to expect.

She stood in front of Curry's house and looked west. The moonlight hit the last of the snow on the peaks of the Big Horns and she expected theme music by Dmitri Tiomkin to swell in her head. It didn't seem possible that this crackerbox house and the mountains were in sight of each other. She wanted a developer to rezone the west and get rid of the trailers and trashy houses and nonphotogenic farms and it would all look like a Saturday matinee starring Joel McCrea. The people who live out here must go inside their ugly houses and look out at the beautiful scenery. Only plaqued buildings on the National Register of Historic Places looked the way they were supposed to, and they were as cold and untouchable as movie sets.

Barb stood beside the pickup with the passenger-door handle in a death grip. She was not going inside. She felt sick and wondered if it was the beer, Curry, or herself. She scuffed gravel. She eyed the dog. She looked through the open door to the living room. Curry opened the screen, which didn't hang plumb, and walked out on the porch. He held two cans of Coors in one hand.

"Igor won't bite you. Come on up."

She wasn't afraid of the dog. He looked like a floppy dust mop, once he collapsed by the porch steps. She didn't want a tussle with Curry, a little ol' roll in the hay. And she didn't know how to get out of it.

Curry had talked steadily through half a dozen Coors and he started repeating himself after two hours. In the pickup she heard about the ticket in Denver again. She was waiting for the rodeo stories to recycle.

She must have sobered up enough on the drive out to realize she was fooling herself. This warm cowboy wasn't really what she wanted. She was being awful. She was disgusted with herself, that she wanted this Jim Bob, that she'd let it go this far.

He'd been out on the ranch, working hard all week. He'd gotten cleaned up, come to town, petted her and danced, chatted and done all the right things, and now she was walking out on the unspoken contract. Bitch. And there was something immovable about him, maybe something he fostered to survive the isolation. People who work alone get strange. When they finally get out and start socializing, they want other people to behave as they expect, as they've imagined in their aloneness. And they are hard when it doesn't happen.

In just two hours she'd become Curry's girl. She laughed at his stories and danced too close and she'd come out here, just the way he planned. She molded herself to him. She'd turned into a cowboy sweetheart because of his pale eyes and his polite manners and heavy shoulders. She didn't know why, but she knew it wasn't going to work.

He sucked on a beer and she clutched the door handle.

"You gonna stay out there all night." He sounded stone-hard-peeved.

"Take me back to town."

"What the hell? You wanted to come here. Now you change your mind?"

"Yes."

"No, you ain't."

"Take me back."

"Not when I had a hard-on for two hours."

"Tough," she said. He'd probably had a hard-on for a week. She turned on her heel and started walking down the long driveway. He caught up with her, grabbed her arm, and spun her around.

"You ain't leaving now."

"It's my period." She shook his hand off.

"No, it ain't."

Barb took a couple of deep breaths. She was weaving a little and things tried to spin. "I'm leaving."

She turned to walk away and Curry hit her hard below the shoulder blades. She flew off balance and hit the dusty red gravel, grazed her chin, and the air whooshed out of her lungs. She wrenched the hand she flung out to catch herself. She was jarred more than hurt. She got to her hands and knees, then to her feet.

She started to say something and he backhanded

Discover a World of Timeless Romance Without Leaving Home

Get
4 FREE
Historical Romances from Harper Monogram.

JOIN THE TIMELESS ROMANCE READER SERVICE AND GET FOUR OF TODAY'S MOST EXCITING HISTORICAL ROMANCES FREE, WITHOUT OBLIGATION!

Imagine getting today's very best historical romances sent directly to your home – at a total savings of at least $2.00 a month. Now you can be among the first to be swept away by the latest from Candace Camp, Constance O'Banyon, Patricia Hagan, Parris Afton Bonds or Susan Wiggs. You get all that – and that's just the beginning.

PREVIEW AT HOME WITHOUT OBLIGATION AND SAVE.

Each month, you'll receive four new romances to preview without obligation for 10 days. You'll pay the low subscriber price of just $4.00 per title – a total savings of at least $2.00 a month!

Postage and handling is absolutely free and there is no minimum number of books you must buy. You may cancel your subscription at any time with no obligation.

GET YOUR FOUR FREE BOOKS TODAY ($20.49 VALUE)

FILL IN THE ORDER FORM BELOW NOW!

YES! *I want to join the Timeless Romance Reader Service. Please send me my 4 FREE HarperMonogram historical romances. Then each month send me 4 new historical romances to preview without obligation for 10 days. I'll pay the low subscription price of $4.00 for every book I choose to keep – a total savings of at least $2.00 each month – and home delivery is free! I understand that I may return any title within 10 days without obligation and I may cancel this subscription at any time without obligation. There is no minimum number of books to purchase.*

NAME_____

ADDRESS _____

CITY_____STATE____ZIP_____

TELEPHONE_____

SIGNATURE _____

(If under 18 parent or guardian must sign. Program, price, terms, and conditions subject to cancellation and change. Orders subject to acceptance by HarperMonogram.)

GET 4 FREE BOOKS
(A $20.49 VALUE)

TIMELESS ROMANCE READER SERVICE

120 Brighton Road
P.O. Box 5069
Clifton, NJ 07015-5069

AFFIX STAMP HERE

her across the mouth. She could taste salty blood and her face hurt.

"What do you do for an encore?" she said. "Kick the dog?"

He stood with fists clenched, watching her. He took a step toward her. She took a breath and vomited. Convulsive spasms bent her double. She hadn't intended to, but she caught Curry, and not just his boots. He backed away. She heard him spit in disgust, but all she could do was stand there and heave till her gut emptied.

When she stopped, she wiped her face and tried to clear her mouth and throat. When she could breathe without triggering a spasm, she straightened up and started down the driveway again. Curry stood with the dog beside the steps.

She was at least two miles out of town, then another mile to the Good Times. She hoped her shoes didn't rub a blister.

This was twice in one night she'd walked out. Or run away. Maybe it was getting to be a habit. She wondered what she was doing, but her thoughts ran in jumbled circles.

Several cars went by, but she was walking against traffic on the yellow-dry grass of the shoulder and nobody stopped. Dusk-to-dawn lights on houses and trailers lit her way over Little Goose Creek, past the Wyoming National Guard building and the community college. It took an hour to get back. The Good Times was still open and she used the ladies' room. Her face was starting to swell and ache. She felt awful. She rinsed and rinsed her mouth over and over, but the taste wouldn't go away. The hand she landed on hurt if she turned it wrong.

By the time she got to her car, she was more or less sober. She fell into the driver's seat, headed for the highway, and wound her way back up to Cloud Peaks.

13

The next day, a Sunday, Barb drove to the Equestrian Club after lunch. She wanted to apologize to Hal. Her mouth was swollen but not discolored. She decided she didn't look too bad. The pain distracted her from what was really bothering her—she had ruined a great friendship.

As if to compensate for the beautiful weather the previous Sunday, it was rainy this week. The wind pushed squalls over the field, making it seem chillier. Clouds masked the mountains and lowered the sky. The light over the foothills was pearly with moisture.

She thought the polo matches began at noon and expected to see a game in progress when she arrived. She asked a woman near the stands and was told they were waiting to see if the rain ruined the field. Barb drove over to the horse trailers, looking for Hal's pickup. She found it, but he wasn't in it. Players with rain gear over their uniform shirts and men in glistening yellow slickers clustered in groups. She spotted Hal by the set of his shoulders and the Montana Peak crease of his hat. The drizzling rain beaded up on the hat brim, then dripped when he moved his head. She waited until he turned and saw her. She tried to read his expression. Grim. Neutral. If he was angry, he wasn't showing it. But he didn't smile, either.

"I came to apologize," she said.

"You have a good time with Curry?"

"Word travels fast."

"You meet Igor?"

"We never established a relationship."

"You and Curry establish a relationship?"

"Do you care?"

He looked disgusted. "Yes. I can't just turn it off. If I'm dating a woman, I care if she sleeps with somebody else."

"I didn't sleep with him." She touched her sore face. It wasn't bruised blue, but it throbbed.

"What happened?"

"I walked out."

"I can't imagine Curry liking that."

"He didn't. Tried to stop me."

Hal looked closely at her face. "Did he hurt you?"

"Not much. I probably deserved it. I didn't behave very well, but I was damned if I'd do something I didn't want to do. I had a nice stroll alone back to town."

"So what do you want with me?" he asked. His expression was as cold as the question was curt.

"Absolution. Penance. Can we talk about this?"

"We did talk. When I told you a little about myself, you walked out."

"That wasn't why." She wanted to cry. She'd hurt him in ways she hadn't intended.

"You want your hat?"

"You got it?"

"In the pickup."

"I guess so." She wanted Hal to hug her and say, "There, there, it's all right." She had stood up and taken her medicine, apologized nicely. But it wasn't going to be that easy.

He got the hat out of the cab of his truck.

She took the hat and put it on. "I wish I could go back to the Golden Steer, eat dinner again, and start over. I'm sorry I ruined things."

"I'm sorry," he said, "for different reasons. I'm not as mad as I was last night, but."

"But what?"

"Nothing. I still don't know why you walked out. We were talking, working things out. Then you just left. No fight, no nothing. Why'd you leave?"

"I don't know. I still don't understand. I just couldn't handle it." Barb tried to think of something wonderful to say, but couldn't. "What did you do?"

"I stayed in the bar and got drunk. I should have gone home, then I wouldn't have heard anything." Hal turned away. Lots of people must have seen her leave the Good Times with Curry, but no one had seen her walk back to town alone. He had been humiliated in front of his friends.

"How long are they going to wait before they cancel or start a game?" she asked.

"Another half an hour or so."

"I'm going to see if there's any coffee in the clubhouse. I'm sorry. I ruined something good. I don't know why I did it. I felt bad. I was confused. When you aren't angry anymore, let me know." She longed to touch him, but he held himself tense and closed and she knew by the sound of his voice that she couldn't.

She got back in her car and bounced over the track around the field to the clubhouse. Coffee didn't help. She got inside the rest room before she started crying.

She cursed herself for a fool, cried for all the good times she'd miss. The worst was losing Hal's calm understanding. She could live without sex, but she wanted his good sense and good humor. She was mad at herself and felt sorry for herself and cried and tried not to make any noise.

She came out with most of her makeup washed away. Now her eyes were red and swollen to match her face. A group of players sat drinking beer at a table. She bought a bottle and walked outside. Drizzle misted lightly through the fly over the deck. She looked over at the pickups and trailers and horses and men at the end of the field. It was foggy over there and the rain muted the colors. She saw yellow slickers and horses being led to rain-shiny trailers.

Okay, Mr. Farrier. I can get along without you. Get tough, Princess, she told herself. Feeling sorry for yourself won't help.

She stood on the clubhouse deck with the beer making her colder and stared at the gray day.

Quentin Maxwell joined her. She recognized

him as one of the players from last week. He wore a spotless red silk shirt and white jodhpurs and carried a beer. He hadn't played yet and Barb wondered about the beer, then remembered that drinking beer wasn't drinking in Wyoming. As near as she could figure, it was like Perrier to a yuppie. If you were drinking seriously, you drank whiskey.

After exchanging names, Maxwell said, "Dismal day."

"Will they cancel?" Barb asked.

"Almost certainly. Don't know what we're waiting around for. The field's too wet."

Maxwell's team—his son and two other players—had won the tournament match the previous Sunday. They played last and by then Barb had caught on a little and could appreciate their skill and energy. She didn't know his handicap, but he was good. She had started making friends with Tony and the wranglers, had gone on to Hal and his friends. She hadn't gotten to know middle-aged people yet, people her own age, like Maxwell. He was stocky and fit with thinning fair hair and a handsome Gaelic profile. He was tanned, of course, and his face creased with smile lines when he talked.

"That was a good game last week," she said. She pulled on her beer.

He smiled. "Yes, we did all right." She remembered him and the others flushed with victory and exertion, standing sweat-soaked outside the clubhouse for the awards after the steeplechase, his son accepting the silver plate. Danny looked a little sheepish, but proud and still excited from the game. She tried to recall what she had heard about Maxwell.

"Do you breed horses?" she asked.

"No, ours is a cattle operation. But of course we have horses. I sell one every now and then."

"Horse trading seems to be a local sport."

He grinned again, and the creases deepened around his mouth.

"I understand you're staying at Cloud Peaks," he said.

"Karen is an old friend. I needed a place to work this summer."

"This isn't the kind of a day we tell tourists about."

"Yes, I thought the skies were not cloudy all day."

"Most days," he said, and looked at thunderheads bunching up against the mountains. "Not this day."

"Will it clear up when the storm moves on?"

"Might. Or it might rain for three days."

"Actually I like it when it rains. The air changes, and the light. It's so dry usually that the rain feels good."

"We had a wet spring. You can still see a little green." He looked past the watered playing field to the rolling foothills. "Usually it starts drying out and everything's brown by now."

Barb had had a dry spring, then felt like she was greening up under the attention of men like Tony and Hal. It felt wonderful after Grimaldi, her drought of the heart. Now she was doing things that weren't getting her what she wanted. It felt like another dry spell.

The president of the polo club pulled up at the clubhouse, got out of his Suburban, and shook his head. He went inside to tell the others the games were canceled.

"Well, that settles it," said Maxwell.

They turned to take their empties inside.

It was pleasant standing there, talking about nothing much. Barb didn't want to go back to Cloud Peaks and count her sins. She wanted to ask Quentin Maxwell what he would do, now that he wasn't going to play polo.

"I'll be looking forward to next week," she said. He smiled and nodded.

Barb actually put a few hours in on Kate Chopin Sunday night, rereading highlighted Xeroxes. She would get the article written and rewritten and revised in spite of herself.

She and Karen didn't set aside any particular time to be together, but because they were both around, they found time to talk—at meals, sometimes in the late-afternoon lull, or before turning in at night.

"Something happened with Hal?" Karen asked as they set the table.

"I messed up."

"It's not the end of the world."

"Promise?"

They both grinned.

One of the girls called Barb to the phone after Sunday-night dinner. She hoped it was Hal and her heart raced.

"This is Quentin Maxwell. How are you?"

Stunned. But she said, "Fine, thanks."

"Would you have dinner with me Tuesday evening? Kelly's in Sheridan has good seafood."

"I thought you were married."

"Not currently. I have appointments Tuesday, lots of business to do, and I thought it would be pleasant to have dinner with you to look forward to."

"Thanks. Yes, I guess. I didn't know." There was silence as the line crackled. "That you were available."

"Would you have acted differently today?"

"Probably."

"What would you have done?" This was flirting, bantering, but he sounded so serious Barb didn't know how to take it.

"I don't know."

"Tuesday at seven?"

"Could we make it six? I'm not sophisticated and I don't like to be hungry and wait."

"I'll remember that. Six, then."

14

Barb continued to read through her material on Kate Chopin. Chopin's private life was astoundingly dull. She appeared to have been happily married, content to be a mother. She looked at writing as something she did in the living room while the children played at her feet. Hardly a feminist theme there, so Barb turned back again to her stories and *The Awakening*, that most perfect novel.

A friend who wrote mysteries once told Barb, "Ten percent falls out and ninety percent you have to push out. But when you get finished, the reader can't tell the difference." When it came to Kate Chopin, nothing was falling out; Barb was pushing every sentence. Once she got going, maybe some momentum would build.

Between her not-very-intelligent search for love, sex, and the meaning of life, and her work on Kate Chopin, Barb hadn't noticed much that was going on at Cloud Peaks. Gradually, now, the kids were taking on personalities. As a teacher, she had seen so many beautiful, intelligent children that it took a while to sort them out. There are too many Kevins and Brians, too many Kathys and Debbies and Kims. Gradually she recognized their individual traits and picked up their humor and they became, as Kelly had, real people.

When her brain went blank around four in the afternoon, Barb even hung out in the kitchen and watched the cook. She asked Lars, the young chef, what ingredients he used and how he did things and he warmed up a little and lectured her about cooking. He was opinionated, with the assurance of youth—he was twenty-four at most. He said capers were useless and refused to cook with them. He hated dates and substituted dried apricots in recipes. He said mothers were bad teachers. He'd learned to cook from his grandma, then went to trade school. Grandmas don't get upset, he said, and there was affection in his voice. They have more patience. They have more time. They teach you the little extra touches.

His apple pie was the best she had ever eaten in her life. He peeled and cut tiny sour apples he picked from a friend's tree in Sheridan, added nothing but sugar and cinnamon. The crust was made with butter and a bit of vinegar in the water. It was still warm when he served it and French vanilla ice cream melted through the vents in the crust. Only a fool would have turned it down. Pies such as that don't come often in a person's life, but now she had tasted bliss.

After a couple of weeks she finally heard the clock chiming by the front desk. The old, polished walnut grandfather clock with the silver face ticked off the hours. It had been there all the time, but the sound hadn't registered.

She discovered there were two kinds of tall evergreens growing around the ranch—lodgepole pine and Douglas fir. For two weeks she had just seen "trees," and not until she noticed the cones, then examined the needles and looked at the bark did she recognize the difference.

While Barb had been absorbed in her own routines Karen and Kirt continued to run Cloud Peaks. Some guests stayed, but most of the first ones left to be replaced by new people. At Sunbelt resorts the pool can lie empty, a turquoise shimmer in the sun. The tennis courts can lie bare, the swept green surface and white lines untouched for hours. The tourists disappear to shop and sightsee. But at a guest ranch there were horses. Each guest was assigned a mount and mornings and afternoons they lined up at the corral while the wranglers saddled up. People who never rode the rest of the year seemed utterly happy to ride twice daily at Cloud Peaks. A wrangler led them out of the park and up mountain trails. Nothing was obligatory or rigidly scheduled—guests could go back to their cabins to nap or read—but there were things to do and people, like Karen and Kirt and Tony, adept at helping people enjoy themselves. A new group of guests would arrive over the weekend and in a few days become friends. Guests gathered around the big fireplace after lunch and dinner to chat. They mixed cocktails, played bridge or board games. One of the wranglers stayed at a cabin higher in the mountains and cooked for pack trips. If a guest wanted a pack trip to fish or photograph, all the food and equipment would be loaded on horses and a guide would lead them into the backcountry. They camped at the cabin. All their needs were taken care of.

The next evening, Monday, there was a beach party. Barb had never had a knack for entertaining and was astounded at Karen's ability to keep the guests happy and occupied. Karen made the wranglers take up the Indian rugs and dump sacks of sand in the main room of the lodge. Barb hated theme parties because they reminded her of kiddie parties where Mummie makes everyone wear funny hats and play dumb games. But she helped Karen put up travel posters for Hawaii and Florida. She planned not to attend, but Karen handed her a grass skirt when she provided costumes for guests. Everyone was told to come to dinner prepared.

They had roast pig, with an apple in its mouth. The cook had trouble repressing a look of pride when he cut through the perfectly browned skin to carve the white, juicy meat. There were melons, fish, and mashed potatoes tinted green, which Lars said was "poi." Barb had helped the girls peel potatoes and, when they were cooked, watched the cook whip them with a big restaurant stainless-steel mixer. He dribbled salted cooking water and pounds of melted butter into the maelstrom. Barb could see he hated to put the green coloring in, but he had a luau menu propped up and he checked it, sighed, and counted the drops of coloring to be swirled in.

The girls and the wranglers showed up in swimsuits. It made Barb cold to look at them. With her grass skirt she wore a tank top and a flowered shirt over that. After dinner Karen, barefoot, wearing a grass skirt, halter, and a plastic lei, led them into the main room. The furniture had been pushed into a corner and screened off. Two battered artificial palm trees incongruously flanked the fireplace and green plastic grass edged the modest sand dunes. Karen turned on the Beach Boys and started serving a near-lethal fruit punch in coconut tumblers. Even Barb got into the spirit of things. She had a flashback of Grimaldi at a Halloween party, leering at her, his Dracula fangs over his lower lip. He had wrapped her in the red-lined costume cloak on the way home and made love with the plastic teeth still in place. Remembering still hurt, but at least she could remember something without crying and admit that not everything had been bad between them.

The girls led hesitant guests into a limbo contest, then everyone got loose enough to dance barefoot in the sand. Tense daddies unwound and their pretty wives danced happily. Kirt danced with single dude ladies, a pair of horse enthusiasts from Long Island, and with Linda, a business executive from Des Moines. Kelly danced with Tony. Two of the wranglers sang the University of Wyoming "Cowboy Joe" song, which Karen said was a Polynesian war chant. Then there was a talent contest. The grayest, most uptight men told the raunchiest jokes. The girls did a skit, which needed many supporting players, and all of them ended up on the floor in the sand. Barb had a great time—laughed, danced with all the men, joined the sing-along around the fireplace.

Then they put on their boots and parkas and went to their cabins.

The morning after the beach party, Barb pitched in and helped the kids sweep up the sand. Kelly held the too-small dustpan as they refilled the double paper sacks. There was one empty sack left over. Where had the sand gone?

As she helped clean up she thought back over the party. She had seen Linda with Kirt but hadn't paid much attention. Other guests couldn't spend enough time riding the mountain trails. They took two pack trips during their stay, coming back grubby and happy, but Linda stayed at the resort, going out twice daily for rides, but otherwise enjoying the other guests and the staff at dinner and in the lodge. Barb learned she was an executive at a regional IBM office with a position of esoteric responsibility—something with computers and traffic. They were of an age, but since they had little in common and since Barb was either thinking of Hal or working on Kate Chopin, she didn't get to know Linda.

Barb still wasn't seeing everything, or she wouldn't have been surprised to find Karen crying in the cabin Tuesday after lunch.

"What's the trouble?" Barb asked, sitting beside her on the couch.

"Nothing." Karen continued to weep and work with the tissue.

"I don't buy that." Barb waited. Karen's eyes were red and her nose redder. Only actresses look beautiful when they cry; the rest of us look crumpled and awful, Barb thought.

"Where's Kirt?" Barb asked.

"That son of a bitch!"

Barb felt as though the chair had been pulled from under her. She had been relying on Karen to take care of her like a good mom.

"He's out with Linda. Again."

Then some odd bits of information fell into place. Linda was amusing herself with Kirt. At least Barb thought that was all it was. She needed Kirt to check her heater, not George. She needed Kirt to give her a riding lesson, Tony wouldn't do. She drew Kirt out in conversation around the big fireplace after dinner.

He usually played the good host, answering questions about the Big Horns and Wyoming and giving the guests a taste of western life. He was attractive, slightly theatrical—the red silk scarf, the flannel shirt. His hat looked authentically abused. Barb knew that he was western, had grown up on a ranch near Kaycee, gone to the state university. But she also knew he had been to K State for graduate school and was the assistant administrator for the Buffalo schools. He owned horses, but he also owned a three-piece suit.

Linda had fallen for his cowboy persona, and he was out to prove it was real.

Now that Barb thought of it, Linda had gotten herself up with a silk flower in her hair and a low halter top at the party and she looked good. She and Kirt had danced a lot.

"What is it this time?" Barb asked.

"They've gone to the gorge. Alone."

Barb remembered the effect that beautiful place had on her when Tony took her there and wondered if Kirt planned to use Tony's tent. And buffalo robe.

"It could be perfectly innocent," Barb insisted.

"He was supposed to come back here after lunch for fun and games with me and he didn't show up. Tony had to tell me where he went."

"Do you want me to talk to him?"

"I'll talk to him. Just wait till I talk to him."

"This is only a dude lady, going home in a few days."

"That's the part that galls me," Karen said. "It's really easy to fall into that routine. 'They're only here for a while and what's wrong with a little fun and it doesn't mean anything.' God, I thought we were better than that."

"Dude ladies have been coming out and falling in love with warm cowboys forever," Barb said. That made her feel funny, since she had done the same thing.

"We agreed we just would not do that," Karen said.

"Does it mean anything?"

"It does to me!" Karen gave her neon nose one last blow. "The last couple who managed Cloud Peaks did a lot of screwing around with guests. Usually Alex, not Martha. More single women come out here alone than men."

"Now I understand the exchange between Tony and Buzzy at the Outlaws."

"What was that?"

"Nothing, just a look, then Buzzy said you and Kirt were good people."

"Well, Kirt just blew it."

"You don't know for sure that they've done anything," Barb said.

"Yes, I do," she replied, very quietly.

Barb didn't know what to say to that. Or what to do. She reached over and gave Karen a squeeze. "What will you do?"

"Confront him. Wait it out. That's the bitch. I don't want to make too much out of it—it'll just get his back up and make it worse."

"So you have to grin and bear it?"

"Not exactly. I'll talk to him tonight."

15

That afternoon Barb got her new summer dress out of the suitcase and pressed it, found a scarf, jewelry. She didn't feel as scared as she had before. She was used to this—middle-aged man, proper invitation. They could talk about books and things she knew something about. It would feel comfortable.

In town, Barb checked the Sheridan County Fulmer Public Library for some information on Kate Chopin, then bought business supplies for her writing projects.

Instead of feeling first-date nervousness she was relatively calm. Then she realized this was the fourth first date. She had made some progress. She had dressed up with nylons and sling pumps for a date with Quentin Maxwell. Would she seduce him?

She walked to The Book Shop to kill half an hour, climbing the stone steps to the old oak-and-glass door set at angles to the sidewalk. There was a big white rattan chair on the tile floor near the front window, and tables, shelves, and even an old iron stove to display books.

Barb felt she was waking up from depression. When she'd had surgery for an ovarian cyst, they gave her shots of Demerol for the pain. Months later places on her backside would tingle and itch, as though damaged nerves were waking up. Since she had been in Wyoming, she had been coming alive, one nerve ending at a time. For example, she must have seen hundreds of acres of sage, but it wasn't until she stopped at one of the parks on the way up to Cloud Peaks that she got close to a clump. Knee-high spears of leaves fanned from a common base. The stalks broke off easily. The smell from the frosted gray-green leaves was clean and heady. She took pieces of sage back to her room and in a day or two they dried brittle. She kept them on her work desk and from time to time crushed a leaf for the smell. Gradually her room took on the scent. But it had been a couple of weeks before she really *saw* the sage, before the damaged nerves came to life.

She found a copy of *The Awakening* for Karen, then picked up another book, walked around a display, and was surprised to find Maxwell there. They laughed and she asked what he was looking for.

"Browsing, finding more books than I have time to read."

"This is a good bookstore for a town this size," she said.

"Yes. A lot of rich people live out here, especially during the summer. They're cultured and can support this store. It's a kind of feudalism."

"What happens when the noblesse oblige runs out?"

He shrugged.

Barb wondered if Quentin Maxwell was cultured. She found a book by Leslie Silko, which she had already read, but wanted to share with Karen. They paid for their books and decided to go on to dinner.

"Which Silko book did you buy?" he asked as they walked to Kelly's.

"*Storyteller*, a new edition. Are you interested in Indian writing?"

"She's more than an Indian writer. I like books about the modern west. They need to be written. People back east don't know anything has happened out here since 1890."

"Who else do you read?" Barb asked. He pulled Thomas McGuane and *The Milagro Beanfield War* out of the sack. Barb nodded. This was one evening she could talk about what she knew. She wouldn't have to feel dumb because she didn't know what a latigo was.

"We were both early," she said.

"You don't like to be hungry and wait," said Maxwell, repressing a smile.

Kelly's was next to the Cody Building on the corner of Main and Alger, with "1907" carved in the stone above the second floor. The scarlet booths and black-and-white-tile floors looked bright, and the smell of good seafood was inviting. The brick walls had been exposed and new brass fixtures installed.

They were the first patrons.

"Well," he said, after he'd ordered drinks, "I wondered if you would accept when I phoned."

"I wondered why you phoned."

"You're an attractive woman."

Barb nodded thanks, then looked at him and said, "Why me? Lots of other attractive women around."

"I don't know. You look interesting. Your face has some character."

She wondered what that meant. More wrinkles? She had been swollen-eyed when they met on the clubhouse porch.

"Quentin."

"Call me Max."

"I'm Barb. English professor out here for the summer. Working on an article. Tell me what you do."

He paused as he flipped through his mental fact file, selecting what to tell her. She wondered how his arms in the well-tailored jacket would feel, wondered what a polo player's legs were like, wondered about his sons, his ranch. They ate the buttery shellfish and exchanged information. Barb was flirty but proper and enjoyed talking about books and opera. It was Culture Hour.

They finished about 7:30. By then every table was filled. That left the rest of the evening.

"I'd like to take you to some quiet bar and talk all evening," Max said as they left.

"I can't think of anything I'd enjoy more." Barb had taken his arm as they left Kelly's and now she squeezed it. "I've spent more time in bars since I got here than I have in years at home. I'm used to inviting people to my house. But out here, that means a long drive up a high mountain."

The summer sun still shone and it would be a long time till dark.

Max looked uncomfortable. "I can't invite you home," he said, and winced. "The boys are there." He hadn't been divorced long enough to face his teenage sons, watching to see what Dad was going to do. "It's a long drive, too, and I've been in town all day as it is."

"I'm disappointed, but I understand. I wanted to get to know you." Barb licked her lower lip. She'd felt lively, making double entendres, playing the courtship game, pressing his hand to make a point. Now the game was canceled. "It was a lovely dinner. Thank you."

"Will you be at the polo games Sunday?" he asked.

"Probably. Do you want me to cheer for you?"

"I thought we might do something Sunday night, afterward."

Barb thought of the first polo Sunday and how she'd gone to Hal's trailer in Story. This wasn't like that. Max didn't look like the type to get carried away by lust. But he was nice and she could use a little nice.

Max walked her to her car and she held out her hand. He shook it, then stared at her. He looked amused, then pulled her tightly against his chest, gave her a quick kiss. Then he released her and said, "Till Sunday," and strode off down the street.

Driving back to Cloud Peaks, she wondered what she was doing. Things had happened so fast.

Was the kiss a pledge or as much as there would be? She'd see what he had in mind next Sunday.

The sunset was gone by the time she pulled into the parking lot. The glassy lake gleamed like mercury, holding the last of the light long after the dark trees had relinquished it. The horses in the corral snorted and she heard their bells jingle.

She walked past the lodge to the cabin and had one foot on the step when she heard Karen and Kirt inside.

"You bastard! You have the nerve to bring her here?"

"Now, Karen, it wasn't what you think."

"What am I supposed to think? Do I have to find you humping her?"

"We were doing no such thing. Where do you get off accusing me?"

"I'm supposed to close my eyes like I'm stupid?" Karen yelled.

"She's just a lonesome dude lady. I was only trying to make her feel at home."

"Don't pull that with me."

"What am I supposed to be pulling?" Sarcasm soaked Kirt's reply.

Dread filled Barb and she wanted to stop them. "Don't do this. You've got too much going for you," she wanted to tell them. She wanted to run away. She tiptoed away from the porch, unable to find steady footing in her heels.

In the lodge she made herself some tea and sat with the group by the fireplace and listened with half an ear to this week's guests talk about what they had seen—baby elk in the park below Cloud

Peaks. One birder jubilantly announced new additions to his life list.

Karen and Kirt needed time alone. If they decided to kiss and make up, she really didn't want to be there. She thought of them making love in the next bedroom and she thought of Hal. She wanted to double over.

Linda sat opposite her on the other couch. She looked perfectly at ease, chatting with one of the guests about sales in her district, sharing some management tips for better interoffice memos. She seemed perfectly capable of finding her own man. Barb had the feeling that Kirt was only a diversion. It might mess up Kirt and Karen, but it wouldn't break Linda's heart. She probably had microchips for a heart.

That's catty, Princess, she told herself.

Barb waited until everyone left the lodge, then turned off the lights and crept back to the cabin. It was dark and silent.

Hearing Karen and Kirt fighting left her with a sick, cold feeling. It wasn't an adult's response to a friend's problem. She couldn't place it until later, as she fell asleep. She was six years old and had just awakened from a bad dream. She wandered into the bathroom, then to the kitchen for a drink of water. But the anguished voices behind the door stopped her.

She heard her daddy's voice, thick with alcohol, accusing and swearing. And Mom cried.

"When you drink, it isn't just a night out, a little escape. It makes me miserable because it's you saying that you don't want to be with us." Then Mom sobbed.

"No, honey, it's not that. It doesn't have anything to do with you." Barb heard him sit heavily and the chair scooted on linoleum.

"It does. I try to make a nice home for you. The girls are clean and well behaved. I'm a good cook. But none of that is enough for you. I work as hard as I can—all the things that need to be done. I don't buy anything I can do myself. All I ask is that you come home."

If Mom did everything right, then he should be satisfied. They were sitting at the Formica table. The much-enameled woodwork and the pink tiles would be spotless, the cutting board bleached white.

"When you're not here, I feel awful. Like I'm only half here." More sobs, then the menacing sound of pans clashing.

"No, no. I love you and the girls."

"Promise you won't do this again," Mom begged.

"I promise." Dad's voice was low and he sounded whipped. He was lying. The time would come when he needed room. When she was little, Barb didn't understand why they fought. She loved them and wanted them to be happy.

But there was always something missing and Dad would look for it and Mom would try harder, meals would get bigger and fussier. The house would be cleaner. Cindy and Barbara would be nagged to look neater, be smarter. They had to do well in school because Mom and Dad made so many sacrifices, and if they didn't appreciate Mom, she cried and accused them of not making her happy.

Barb had never gotten used to wrinkled, all-cotton clothes. She'd spent too many hours trying to look perfect. Other people were criticized for being dirty, unladylike, cheap. She and Cindy studied hard, that went without saying. They both got scholarships. Cindy found Sid before she graduated, but she graduated before they got married. Barb just kept going to school.

Barb grew up thinking she had to be perfect or her man would leave. She wasn't and he did. Karen and Kirt fighting in the cabin washed away the grown-up and she was six years old again, standing outside the kitchen door, hearing voices and feeling small and sad.

The next morning at early breakfast Barb interrupted something at the kids' table and knew they had been talking about Linda and Kirt. The resort was such a tight little society that nothing escaped notice. Or comment.

At the regular breakfast Karen presided blandly. Barb went to work at her typewriter and didn't see Karen until later. Karen sat at the front desk, writing.

"What happened?" asked Barb.

"Where were you?"

"I heard the sounds of battle when I got back last night and withdrew."

"Wise of you."

"Well?"

"He wouldn't admit anything."

"What are you going to do?"

"Nothing."

"Just nothing?"

"I'm not going to snoop around or keep tabs on

him. If that's what he wants to do, I'm not going to stop him. I'm not going to like it, either. He knows that."

"You can't just let these years go for nothing!"

"You did."

"I didn't have a choice. And I wasn't there to fight back."

"She's only here for three more days."

"And you're going to grin and bear it? That's not like you."

Karen rubbed her face and took a deep breath that wasn't quite a sigh. "It's up to him. I made it clear. If he keeps it up with Linda or tries it again, I'll divorce him. It only takes three weeks in Wyoming."

"I can't believe it."

"I can't, either. But that's what I said." She stared bleakly at the door, then pulled her yellow pad over and picked up the pen. "So now I'm waiting."

16

Later that week Karen asked, "What happened with you and Quentin Maxwell?"

"It was very nice." Barb was touched that Karen could be interested when her own affairs were up in the air. "Dinner at Kelly's. We talked about opera in English, new western writers, local politics."

"It must have felt familiar."

"It did, now that you mention it. Comfortable. I wonder why?"

"For an otherwise intelligent person, sometimes you can be awfully dense," Karen said, and smiled.

"What do you mean?"

"Max isn't your warm cowboy," she said. "Nothing like Hal Simmons."

"True."

"He's Grimaldi in cowboy boots."

"No!"

"Sure. Middle-aged, respectable, cultured, nothing to excess. Boring."

— 152 —

LOVE WITH A WARM COWBOY 153

"It was familiar."

"What happened to you last Saturday?"

"A close encounter of the worst kind. With Curry Cannon."

"How did you hook up with him?"

"Long story. About a hat. I walked out on Hal." When she said it, an anvil fell on her chest and she crossed her arms to hold herself together. She wanted Hal, and when she thought of him and her body reacted, it hurt because she couldn't have him. It reminded her of how stupid she'd been, and insensitive. And how much she missed Hal.

"Tony, Hal, Curry, Max. You've been a busy girl."

"Too busy. I want something calm, like Quentin Maxwell."

Barb arrived at the Equestrian Club on Sunday in time for Max's match. She saw Hal drinking beer and talking with friends, then he disappeared. She felt rotten. A friend of Karen's introduced herself and they chatted during the match. Vira knew horses and knew polo and Barb enjoyed learning as she watched. She still had trouble getting beyond the aesthetics of the game—the color and movement, the grace and action. She'd have had to grow up with horses to know as much as Vira or Max or Hal. She loved the wind whipping her hair and the sun on her back as she sat there in the stands. She longed to find Hal, touch him, wrap her arms around him, smell his healthy body. She wanted to brush away what she'd done to hurt him.

She'd think about Max instead.

After the games she joined Max at the clubhouse. He beamed when Danny accepted the silver trophy for another team.

They sat at a table with a polo-player friend and his wife and their guest from Vermont and had a drink. It was fun to watch the players like Max and his friend. They'd gone all out for a couple of hours, changed horses two or three times, and they'd enjoyed themselves. Max explained that there were no set teams, that players switched around every week so new players had a chance to play with more experienced ones. "You don't get better if you can't play with and against someone better," he said. That must have been part of the reason it seemed so relaxed. These people were playing for fun, not just to win.

Barb caught the vibrations that team players send out after a game. A kind of eye contact and occasional slap on the shoulder, grins as they recalled some incident. Shared accomplishment, shared experience.

Max excused himself, got his bag from the car, and went to shower.

Barb saw Hal standing with a group from Terrell's ranch. He looked up and saw her, nodded, grim-faced. Longing for him grew. She gave him a dazzling smile and touched the brim of her hat with a shaky hand. Be nice, she thought. It will disarm some and confuse the hell out of others. She shared dude notes with the man from Vermont, warned him about sunburn. He was still feeling the effects of the altitude and she realized that after two-plus weeks she had gotten used to it. Max returned dressed in tailored cotton slacks, a knit shirt, and navy blazer, his hair wet-combed. He smelled faintly of Brut.

"Where's your car?" he asked.

"What about Danny and the horses?" she asked.

"Danny can get the horses home himself."

"Where are we going?"

"Party in Sheridan." He was still on his players' high and swept her out to the parking area. He wrote directions, but she insisted he draw a map. Barb had spent too much time driving in Wyoming thinking she was lost when she wasn't. She left first, drove into Sheridan, up the hill, left at the hospital, then past the fairgrounds and through the subdivision to a comfortable house. Volvo station wagons and pickups filled the street. Max pulled in behind her a few minutes later. A buffet dinner was just beginning on the patio.

This was familiar—older people, socializing at home.

Barb met several teachers, a visiting historian from one of the Montana universities, a lawyer, and some other business friends of Max. Karen was right; she was back in Kansas City. It was educated, professional, middle class, proper. It was almost too much like what she'd left behind. The house was suburban good taste with one museum-quality Navaho hanging on the living-room wall and an impressive collection of Papago baskets. They talked books and local politics and Sheridan Arts Council and the Grand Teton Symphony. She was comfortable. Then someone began talking about pornography and Barb spoke up.

"I think the First Amendment ought to be the

Eleventh Commandment. I don't think anything should be forbidden to adults. First it's naughty stuff the censors call pornography, then it's political ideas they call dangerous. Who knows where it will end? There was an antiporn campaign in Kansas City that raised a lot of money. Turned out there were already statutes against kiddie porn and that the laws were enforced and violators convicted. The group was trying to invent the wheel. And all the money just went to keep the organization going so it could raise more money."

"I disagree," said Max. "You put that filth where grown-ups can buy it and kids buy it, too. We don't need that kind of stuff in the Mini Marts."

"Next you're going to say it leads to the dissolution of the nuclear family," Barb said.

"I don't know about that. I just know I don't want it where Danny and Ellis can get it."

She had to respect him for that. Maybe if she had kids, she'd think differently.

"You can't legislate morality," she countered. "You can keep the porn mags out of the stores where kids can't get it, and it just goes underground. I think it's disgusting, but I will fight for the right for someone to be able to read what he wants."

Max frowned. "Let it go underground. Make it that much harder to get."

"Anything forbidden is more desirable," Barb said. She studied his weathered face and clear eyes as he talked. His brief kiss on Tuesday had made her curious for more. He was stuffy but attractive, definitely attractive. He seemed almost delicate because of his green eyes and the pink flush of his fair skin. His hair was thin and fine as baby hair, the scalp shining and clean. She didn't particularly like the smell of Brut, but wondered what the combination of Max and Brut would be like.

She sat near him and listened as he spoke. When they were alone in the kitchen getting coffee, he took her in his arms. His kiss was thoughtful, gentle, and exploratory. She felt the ready warmth spread inside and relaxed. Sweet smooching in the kitchen, domestic and comfy. They returned to the party carrying coffee cups. She brimmed with anticipation.

They left the party together as darkness fell. Another spectacular sunset spilled over the mountains, sapphire and amethyst and rose, filling the air with crimson the color of Indian paintbrush. She waited for him to suggest something and finally asked, "Would you like to go to the Holiday Inn for another drink?"

"The disco bar is awful," he said.

"We can have a drink in the lobby, listen to the waterfall. We could talk about ourselves." They reached her car.

"And what would we talk about?" he asked.

"Whether to keep it platonic."

"I think we better." He looked away, then ducked his head. "I'm sorry, Barb. It just isn't working."

She wanted to say, "It's working for me." She swallowed and tried to think of something bright to say. She'd asked for this, up front. She could feel a replay begin of all the Grimaldi-induced bad feelings. Stop it, Princess, she ordered herself. Don't you think you've run that into the ground?

She'd risked a little. So this was what it was going to be like. You try it on and see if it fits. If it doesn't, you don't spend weeks kicking yourself. You don't assume something's wrong with you. You pick yourself up and smile.

"Max, I'd rather spend hours just talking with you than I would with anyone else I've met since I came out here. I've had a great time. I wish it worked."

"Hell, so do I, but I'm not very good at faking it."

Was that what she was doing? She wrapped an arm around his waist. "It's been fun."

The drive up to Cloud Peaks was beginning to seem shorter. Once she passed the snowmobile parking lot, she counted on the drive to smooth her anxieties. She had gotten into the habit of spacing out, not quite the interstate trance, but operating on the right side of the brain until traffic or a bad road woke her up. The foothills fell away behind her, their curves graceful as a dancer's arabesque, lines supple and achingly beautiful. Then she drove up into tall, straight pines, past lily-pad ponds, tumbled boulders. The light changed and the colors faded until she could only see ocher gravel ruts in the headlights.

She had backed out when it was down and dirty with Curry, and Max had backed out when it was clean and nice. She'd never figured out what she had done with Hal.

But he was on her mind. He wasn't as polished as Max. He was ardent. He was kind. And she was mad as hell at him. Why hadn't he stopped her? Why had he let her walk out of the bar and get herself in trouble? Why hadn't he made her face her confusions and work them out?

That was absurd.

The next morning she sat down at the typewriter after breakfast and didn't get up until she finished the first, rough draft of the Chopin article. Tuesday morning she began class notes for Victorian Literature by Women. She had read everything, annotated it, made notes, but hadn't divided the material into classes week by week for the syllabus. Once that was done, she began typing lecture outlines.

Wednesday evening she wandered out of the cabin late in the afternoon for some fresh air and saw Linda dressed to leave. One of the wranglers loaded her expensive, matched luggage into the van.

"It was nice meeting you," Linda said, and held out her hand.

"Yes, me too," said Barb.

"You're a friend of Karen's, aren't you?"

"Yes. We go back to college."

Linda looked over the lake, taking in the trees and the mountains one last time. "I never thought when I came out here that cowboys were interesting. I just wanted to get away from the telephone."

Barb nodded.

"Kirt seemed nice. I thought it would be fun. I think I fell in love with his scarf and boots and hat."

"I can understand that." Barb had fallen for callused hands and strong shoulders and blue eyes that pulled in the green of the grass.

"He was nice and I haven't met anybody like that for a while." Linda smiled and one side of her mouth went up further than the other, as though it weren't a real smile.

Why was she telling Barb this? Barb didn't even like her, but she didn't seem quite the Dragon Lady just now.

"I made a play for Kirt and it worked. For a while. Then he caught himself. I can't believe it's only been a few days."

Linda was looking out over the reservoir to the peaks, not really talking to anyone.

"I've never been turned down so sweetly. I almost didn't feel it when I hit the ground. He said, 'If I did this kind of thing, you'd be the one I'd do it with.' Said I deserved someone who could get involved." Linda's big brown eyes teared up and she stopped.

What could Barb say? She felt sorry for Linda. She was beautiful and made lots of money, but she couldn't have her warm cowboy. Maybe she would go back to Des Moines and find someone like Kirt, now that she knew what she wanted. She turned toward the van and Barb impulsively hugged her. Linda started, then hugged back.

After the van pulled out, Barb walked around the reservoir. The sky was just beginning to color. She thought she'd burn out on Wyoming sunsets, but the sky kept putting on a different show every time. She stuck her hands in her jacket pockets.

You can have anything you want badly enough, Princess. You just have to decide what it is.

She thought of Grimaldi, the ghost of bad feelings past, and Tony with the buffalo robe, and Curry, the Jim Bob Who Failed.

She knew what she wanted; she wanted Hal. And she knew what she had to do.

17

The next morning Barb phoned Terrell's ranch.

"Is Hal Simmons working at your place today?" she asked.

"No, he finished here Friday," said Mrs. Terrell.

"Do you know where he is?"

"I think he said something about going to Clearmont."

"Whose ranch?"

"Walker's, I think."

"Thanks," said Barb.

She verified Hal would be at Clear Creek and asked the Cloud Peaks cook to pack some sandwiches and fruit and a Thermos of coffee. She'd provide the humble pie. She numbed herself out on the music from the car radio, cranked it up really loud so she got inside the music. When she started to think about what she was doing, she turned her attention back to the radio so she wouldn't scare herself out of doing it. She heard Sunday's polo results.

Barb had never faced her stupidity this way before. She was afraid—trembling and stammering scared. What if she made an absolute fool of herself for nothing? She was opening herself up for a kick in the face. No, Hal wouldn't be mean. She was letting him know how much she wanted to be with him and that made her feel shaky and weak. She swerved, hit the gravel, and cursed the lack of shoulders on the state roads. Then she pulled off the asphalt to the two miles of gravel, splashing through soupy red mud from last night's rain.

She parked behind the Walkers' house, went in, and introduced herself to Sarah Walker, then made her way to the corral, where she could see Hal's pickup. Several men clustered around a horse tied to a plank of the corral fence. The top plank looked chewed, as though horses teethed on it. She waited until they released that horse, then walked over to Hal.

Her heart was in her throat, where she was choking on it. She tried to lick her lips, but her tongue was dry. She picked her way down the path. Why was she here? What was she doing? She wanted Hal to say, "There, there, it's all right," and stroke her back so she'd quit feeling like a bitch, crazy and disconnected. She was eager and confused and worried, as though someone had told her she won the lottery, but she had to figure out how to claim the prize. Then Hal saw her and put down his tools and leaned against the fence, apparently relaxed, but there was something about the angle of his shoulders or the bend of his knee that told her it was a pose.

"Hi," said Barb.

"What are you doing here?" he asked. His voice was so low she could barely hear him. He scowled.

"I want to talk to you."

"I'm busy."

"You've got to stop for lunch sometime."

"I'm eating at the house."

"I've got a picnic. I'll be waiting in your pickup."

"What if I don't want you in my pickup?"

"I'll still be waiting."

He turned back to his bench, selected a shoe from the supply in the truck, and motioned for Doug Walker to bring another horse over.

She wished she could calm the sweats and slow her heartbeat. She wasn't nearly as tough as she talked. She got the lunch basket from her car and sat on the shady side of Hal's cab. She checked herself in the mirror, then tried to settle down. She heard Mrs. Walker call that lunch was ready, then Hal stopped at the truck and motioned that he was going to wash up.

"What's going on?" he demanded in a tight voice when he returned. He sounded so controlled it was scary, as though his turnbuckle were too tight. His eyes, usually sky blue, were dark and hard, shaded by the brim of his old hat.

"I want to apologize and explain, if I can," Barb said.

"Don't bother."

"I'm sorry I hurt you. I got crazy. I want to make up."

He didn't say anything, just sat gripping the steering wheel. She dug into the basket and brought out a thick roast-beef sandwich on crumbly homemade bread. He shook his head.

"I thought we were getting along okay," he said. "I was feeling fine, like we had a good thing going. Then"—he pounded the steering wheel and she jumped—"you walked out with no warning. Just like Julie."

"Who's Julie?"

"My ex-wife."

"That's not fair. I'm not your wife and I don't know what she did."

"I didn't want a divorce. I still loved her. But she wanted out. When I wouldn't quit trying to make it work, she walked out, started an affair with her boss, and made sure I knew about it."

"Sounds painful," Barb said.

He shrugged.

"Did it work?" she asked.

"Did what work?"

"She wanted out and you wouldn't let go, so she shocked you into letting go. Did you agree to the divorce then?"

"Yes. I never looked at it like that."

"And I walked out like she did."

"You walked out."

"What can I say? I did it and it was crazy and wrong and I abused your good nature and screwed up."

"Then you take up with Curry, that slob."

"Not exactly."

"Then Sunday I saw you with Maxwell."

"We went to a party."

"Are you going to sleep with every man who asks you out?"

"That's not fair!" Barb clenched her fists so she wouldn't rake his face. She felt each fingernail punch the palm. She was on edge with too many strong emotions—longing and anxiety and fear and regret. "That's cheap! That's not true! You don't know that I went to bed with either of them." She threw the passenger door open, slid out of the pickup, and stood, breathing hard, in the sun.

"Get back in here," he said.

She tried to breathe, slowly climbed back in the cab.

"I don't *care* if you do it with every man in Buffalo County, but I would like to know what happened with us."

"You *do* care."

He looked at her as if she'd stabbed him and he turned away. She was glad because she couldn't stand to see the open hurt on his face. His accusations came out of that hurt and it made her weak because that's how Grimaldi made her feel and she knew it was lousy. And she'd done it to someone else.

"I care about you," she said. "I just can't understand what I did. At the time it made perfect sense."

That stopped him. He turned to face her.

"You saw how shaky I was," she continued, "and you treated me gently." She looked at his face. That was her punishment, to see him hurting. She leaned away from him and bent to take the Thermos out of the basket.

"Why are you saying this?" he asked.

"Because I'm trying to figure out what I'm doing, too."

Hal shifted in the car seat. His boots tapped the pedals. She felt like running away, but if this was what she wanted, she had to finish it. She opened the Thermos and poured coffee. She spilled some when she put the Styrofoam cups in the holder.

"Let's return to the scene of the crime, Watson," she said. She tried to keep her voice light. "We bought this hat I'm wearing." She tugged it down firmly. "We had dinner. You teased me, told me you'd been to college, told me about your little girl."

Hal glanced over at her, then looked away.

"I tried to pick a fight and you were too good-humored to go along with it. I started feeling bad, trying to find something wrong. Called you on contraceptives. Then I wished I had never met you."

Hal looked at her, puzzled. She picked up the coffee, but her hand was shaking, so she put it down, like the drink on the deck the day she met Andrija. She'd never fool anyone with a show of aplomb as long as the shakes gave her away.

"Stay with me, I think I'm getting it," she said. She turned toward him. His hair curled around his ears and his mustache looked dusty. He had dirt on his shirt sleeves.

"If being with you felt this good, *does* feel good. And I liked you this much. And I might grow to love you. Then when I have to leave at the end of the summer, I'll feel worse than I did when Grimaldi trashed me. And I'll be doing it to myself." She fiddled with the button on the glove box until the door fell open.

"So you'd been hurt and now you were going to stop things so you wouldn't feel bad again?" Hal looked at her, puzzled. Then he said, "Do you want something in there?"

She slammed the glove box closed. "You notice I'm not always as smart as I think I am."

She thought she saw him smile a little.

"That's what keeps you from being impossible," he said. "You're not afraid to admit you don't know something."

Barb smiled then.

"It was like a rubber band," she said. "I arrived here all clenched up. I started to unwind. I found you and started getting some of my nerve back, started feeling like life went on. All the bad stuff faded."

"So, why?"

"The rubber band snapped back."

It was painful to say those things, to remember Grimaldi, to realize she'd fallen into one of her old routines where she expected to get kicked. Her eyes teared up and she wished she didn't have to blow her nose or wonder if her mascara was running. She felt rotten. He didn't understand and she had put herself through this for nothing.

"I didn't think I deserved it," she continued. "Deserved you. Maybe I just can't face it. You said, do what you want and take responsibility for it. Drive drunk and take the DUIs. Well, I don't want to take the consequences. Somewhere down the line I'll have to pay for feeling good."

"That doesn't make sense," Hal said.

"It doesn't," she agreed.

They both stared out the window at the sage-dotted hills through the dust Walker's horses stirred up.

"So I ruined a good thing. And I'm sorry." She couldn't hold the tears in any longer and they ran down her face and she licked them at the corners of her mouth. She was emptied and exhausted, as if she'd been digging ditches for hours. "What's going to happen now?"

"Do you want to try again?" he asked.

"Yes." It came out in four syllables.

"I'm afraid to get into it. I'll never know when you'll snap back again," he said. She cringed.

"I won't know if you'll change, either, dammit. If you'll find someone else. What I thought was sure with Grimaldi wasn't. It never is sure. I'll always be afraid you'll walk out. Like Marty. Like Julie."

"I need to think about this," he said. He leaned toward her and pulled a sandwich out of the basket on the floor.

"Maybe we can meet and just talk," she suggested as she opened a Baggie of grapes. She couldn't swallow a sandwich.

"I'm going to Fort Collins next week. Shoeing workshop and I've got friends there."

"Call me when you get back. Let me know one way or another."

"All right." He tossed the half-eaten sandwich back in the basket and finished his coffee. She wanted some reassuring touch, but was afraid to reach for him. He slid out of the cab and walked to the ranch house. She watched his hard ass in his faded Levi's and the straight, tense line of his shoulders. He was so stiff his arms didn't swing. But she loved the way he moved, his rhythm and his unconscious grace.

18

That week at Cloud Peaks one girl left and another came down with the awful stomach flu, and Karen and the housekeeper had to pitch in to keep things running smoothly. Somehow Karen and Kirt made sure everything for the guests got done. They didn't talk to Barb about their relationship.

Karen planned Christmas in July, so Barb volunteered to drive to Sheridan for things Karen needed. When she had scratched everything off the shopping list, she headed out Coffeen, then decided to take the state highway to Story. When she got to the fork, she looked at the sign and turned up into the foothills of Story instead of heading for Buffalo and Cloud Peaks.

She parked in front of Hal's trailer. She stared at his front door. She wanted to go in, lie down on his bed, open his closet, absorb his molecules. He was in Fort Collins. She knew his door wasn't locked. She could just go in.

And she knew that was too much.

Princess, how about a chorus of "On the Street Where You Live"? Are you going to write his name in your civics book?

She knew he could use a secretary to clean up his paperwork. Might even be grateful.

No! That was his space and she had no right to intrude.

Reluctantly she started her car, turned around, and made her way to Cloud Peaks.

The next day Barb and Kelly cleaned toilets and made beds and prayed that the two girls now down with flu would recover and that they wouldn't catch it. The mindless, automatic movements lulled her.

Hal phoned Friday night.

"Let's go to the Tunnel Inn," he said. "And talk."

Two draft horses hitched to an open wagon stood outside the log building of the restaurant, in a row with parked cars. Hal and Barb walked inside, past the bar and into a room on the right. Pink tablecloths and rose napkins were laid on a dozen or so tables of different sizes and candles flickered in glass globes. Antique collectibles, paintings, and posters decorated the walls and the menu was no-nonsense. As they ate he told her of Fort Collins and she told him about her syllabus and shared gossip from Cloud Peaks. They avoided any personal topic. She longed for him to say they'd get back together, but she couldn't push it.

"I wasn't expecting to miss you," Hal said, when the coffee came.

"I wanted you to."

"Now I don't know what to say."

"Say whatever you want."

He stared into his coffee for a while, drank some, looked at her. She was numb. She stared at the Owl Room at the back. She had been holding herself in, not letting her expectations rise, not letting herself feel much of anything. Anticipation hung like a raindrop on the end of a fir needle. She wondered if he still was leery of her, afraid she'd snap back again.

"When Julie walked out on me, it was a big shock. When you just got up and left the Mint Bar that night, it brought all the bad feelings back."

"Tell me about it."

"Hell, I never think about that. It was nasty, but I got through it and it doesn't bother me anymore."

"Yes, it does."

He tightened up and looked away. She waited. She wasn't going to be any bogeyman. "Don't tell me anything you don't want to," she said. "Friends tell each other their stories. All I've done is cry and talk about myself and apologize. I don't know what you care about or how you feel about very many things."

"I'll just tell you the facts, how's that?"

"Go ahead."

"I was finishing up my degree in animal husbandry at Colorado State," Hal said. "I'd worked my way through, waiting tables winters and working on the ranch where my folks live during the summers. Julie and I hit it off, the way two people do, and we were carefree students, fucking and having a good time. Then I graduated and I didn't get into the vet school, so I thought I'd hang around while Julie finished up, take some graduate courses, and apply again. We moved in together and she said she couldn't get pregnant, that there was something wrong with her tubes. But two months later there was nothing wrong, because she was pregnant.

"It was dumb, I guess, to just take her word for it, but I wasn't sorry she was pregnant. We got married right away. I thought her dad would meet me at the state line with a twelve-gauge shotgun, but they were nice, considering I'd knocked up their only little girl. I quit graduate school, worked full-time. I loved it. Julie was beautiful then. She was beautiful, anyway. She had thick black hair down to her waist and rosy skin, and those months she glowed like a lamp in the dark. She got bigger and bigger and we made up new positions, new ways to make love. It was great."

Hal's face glowed, too, as he remembered the good times. Barb nodded, but said nothing. He didn't need prompts.

"Then Mary Louise was born and that was the most powerful thing, the strongest emotion, I can't express it. It moved me more than anything, any experience I ever had. Just thinking about it. I was there, coaching, and breathing, and then at the end, when it was hard for Julie, I couldn't do anything. And the little head came out, and pretty soon the rest of her, and we had a little girl. I'd forgotten what a thrill that was."

He pulled a handkerchief out of his back pocket and blew his nose.

"She was a great baby, after we got her to sleep through the night. She'd coo and grab my finger and it seemed like she was the first baby to ever do those things. I got up with her during the night and changed her and gave her baths.

"I got this job in Casper, working for a big construction company, one that had contracts for highways. I wrote programs so they knew what material they had on hand and what they needed and where and when it had to be there. It was pretty interesting. Julie got bored staying home and I wasn't making that much, so she started substitute teaching and then she worked full-time as a paralegal. Mary Louise went to day-care. I took her in the morning and picked her up at night. I spooned baby goo into her and played peekaboo and changed diapers.

"This is going to sound corny, but I don't think I could love Mary Louise as much if I hadn't done all those things for her.

"I thought everything was okay. Mary Louise was growing up, almost three. I'd gotten a promotion. Julie and I weren't as wild in bed and we argued over things, like did we need a bigger TV or should we go to Jackson to ski or wait and go to California in the summer. We weren't perfect, but, hell, that's life. You can't be carefree students forever.

"Then, out of nowhere, she says she wants a divorce."

He stopped as if the shock hit him for the first time.

"She just said it wasn't fun anymore. I wouldn't move out. I insisted we go for counseling. We went, but she wasn't interested in making it work. She wasn't mad or resentful or hurt. She didn't seem to feel anything at all. We didn't fight, but we didn't make love, either. I felt like I was flaking apart. I couldn't hold the pieces together."

Hal looked hurt and angry and desperate. His voice hummed with misery. She wanted to comfort him, but couldn't do anything to change the past. He sat in silence for a long time and she wondered if he was going over it all again. At last she said, "Trying to figure out what went wrong?"

"Yes," he said, and looked at Barb. "Julie said I didn't talk enough. I tried to talk, but it's easier for me to do something than say something. She said I wasn't sensitive to her needs. I told her to teach me what she wanted, but I was supposed to know everything already. Hell, my dad called my mother darlin' and expected dinner on the table at six every night and he never told her how much money we had or what he spent it on. They got along all right. But Julie wanted more consideration. I tried—hell, I tried until I felt like my brain was bleeding, but it wasn't enough. I was what she wanted when we started. What she wanted changed and I was still me.

"I would have done anything to stay with Mary Louise. God, I love that kid. I did housework, laundry, whatever. I'd take her to the park. I built her a play set in the yard. Then Julie packed up and left. I came home from work one day and her clothes were gone, all of her things from the bathroom. And Mary Louise's things.

"I went in the kitchen and just sat there, numb. There was a note on the fridge. She said she was staying with her boss, this attorney, and she gave the number. I phoned and she answered. That's when she said she wasn't just staying there, she was getting married."

He shook his head. "I still don't know what went wrong."

"Probably nothing. She just wanted out."

"You didn't stay numb forever. What did you do?"

Barb told him how she went crazy, stomped the car.

"You punched out your car?"

"Yes," she said. "See this place on my hand? It's still sore. I kicked in the doors and jumped on the hood till it caved in, then I jumped on the roof till I fell off."

"Can't believe Ms. Professor did something like that."

"I can show you the bill from the body shop. What did you do?"

"I got drunk every night. Found some good buddies and we closed the bars in Casper. Except when I was going to see Mary Louise the next day. Those Saturdays and Sundays were all I lived for. Every time she asked why I didn't live with them anymore, I couldn't talk. 'Why you cry, Daddy?' I'd pick her up and put her on my shoulders so she couldn't see my face.

"Then there were lawyers and the divorce was fast. Julie didn't marry her boss. You said she just did that because I wouldn't get the message otherwise? You're right. I would never have quit trying. I couldn't believe she'd just go from me to him and decide so fast."

He sounded as though he still couldn't believe it. Barb wondered what Julie wanted that Hal couldn't provide. Or couldn't be. He drank off the last of his coffee and stared.

"People think that the father is cold when he moves away from his kids after a divorce. I couldn't stand to be that close to Mary Louise and not be able to see her. I couldn't kiss her good night or pour her Cheerios or take her to day-care. It was tearing me apart."

Barb brushed tears off her cheeks. She didn't want him to stop until he was finished.

"I just left. I talked to my dad and he said they needed a farrier on this big Montana ranch. I'd done some shoeing and I talked to the boss. Took a course and worked for them for a year. Then I came down here and went in business for myself. This is closer to Casper. The worst part is, some housekeeper who doesn't love Mary Louise is doing what I did, pulling her shirts over her head, cutting up her meat at dinner, taking her temperature when she's sick, seeing her every day, doing the things I want to do. Damn."

"So that's where you hurt," Barb whispered.

"One of the places."

"What else?"

"Shoeing is okay for now, but I can't do it forever. It's hard and it's boring. I need to find something I can do the rest of my life, pay child support, and leave enough so I can—" He stopped.

"Start another family?" she asked.

"Yes, someday."

"You make me wish I had a child. I didn't know men felt that strongly about their kids."

"This one does."

"You're just as intense as I am. You move slower and you talk slower and seem calmer. But we both have the same emotions." She searched to describe the feeling. "We resonate on the same key."

"We have something in common, some kind of hunger."

"So we responded to each other without knowing why, on intuition."

"I guess." He shrugged.

"Are you all right?" she asked. "I didn't mean for you to feel bad."

"No, I haven't talked about it with anyone. I needed to look at what happened and face it."

"It's hard," she said.

"So when you walked out, it was more than just leaving the Mint Bar. I've never gotten used to being walked out on."

"I don't think you ever do." Barb had to clear her throat. "I didn't mean to tear open the sore places by walking out."

"Well, I guess I could have taken it a little calmer. We had a good thing going. I like you. Maybe I'm in love with you. Maybe it's lust. Whatever it is, let's give it a try again."

It took a minute for that to sink in, then she smiled and took a deep breath.

"Let's take it slow and see what happens," he said.

"Sounds fine," she said, and managed to keep

her voice steady. She took another deep breath. When she let it out, her hands started trembling like a rock climber who's been hanging from a half-inch ledge too long.

"I'm afraid I'll snap back, too," she said. "You may have to wait out some craziness again."

"Maybe this time I won't take it personally." His blue eyes were dark and he fiddled with the coffee spoon. "One thing."

Her heart beat double time.

"What's that?" Her voice came out breathy and cracked on the second word.

"Let's not take it slow."

She smiled and reached across the table to take his hand again. Hers was shaky; his was warm and dry and the calluses were rough. The second and third fingers bent sideways, as though they'd been broken. He took her hand and they looked at each other. The warm rush began to fill her up.

"You in a hurry to get back to Cloud Peaks?" he asked.

19

As they drove back from the Tunnel Inn the sun shone for them and the street was paved to take them where they wanted to go. Everything seemed possible. The heavy green of the Douglas firs reached into the foothills where Hal steered the pickup through winding Story roads.

When they got to his trailer, they hurried inside in silence, then kissed in the living room, groping and tasting as though they were starved. Their clothes flew through the air. Longing made Barb's gut cramp. Then he touched her, skin to skin, and she shuddered and pulled him to her. Then the bed, bursts of pleasure, touching, feeling.

"You going to shower?" he asked, sometime during the night. It was dark out and Barb didn't remember the sun setting. She had slept and wakened.

"Yes. Join me?"

"I can't move."

She laughed, full of that honeymoon feeling of being complete. But like that cold day in August that reminds you November will come, she was afraid it wouldn't last. Something would happen and the equipoise would shatter.

The next morning they ate canned chicken noodle soup and crackers for breakfast—that's all there was in the trailer. They were tippy-toeing around, afraid the talk would get too close to the bone. All super-polite, careful. Lust got them back in bed, but they hadn't taken care of the rest of the friendship.

Barb walked out the trailer door and Hal said, a little too fast, "Where're you going?"

"To my car. I need something." Hal's calm was usually unshakable. They'd both go nuts if he was going to twitch every time she went anywhere.

She could use his toothpaste and deodorant, but he had no lotion and the fine, clean air dried her face like a deerskin nailed to the side of a barn. The sunscreen she kept under the driver's seat would have to do.

She didn't know how to handle the situation. It would be uncomfortable and they would work it out and they would get used to it and then it would be okay. They did like each other. They did want to be together. They were just jumpy.

Barb came back inside and said, "We can't live like this. I'm afraid something I say is going to spook you. You can't wonder if I'm going to split every time I leave the room."

"I was feeling the strain," he admitted.

"So what now?"

"Go slow."

They sat on the couch with the sag in the middle and she buried her nose in the hollow of his collarbone and breathed in the faint smell of soap and skin that was his. She rubbed his battered hands, with the bent fingers and the calluses, as though she were rubbing a stone. His body accommodated hers. There was a place inside his arm where she fitted, shoulder into his armpit, his arm around hers, ribs together—a tectonic-plate fit, as though they had been cut from the same continent; it took both of them to make it whole.

"How do you feel?" she asked.

"Not waiting for the snap. Relaxed."

She flinched. "That was mean."

He squeezed. "You?"

"Content," she said.

Barb went back to Cloud Peaks Friday night for clean clothes and her own shampoo. Hal planned for something she thought was team roping at the Sheridan fairgrounds Sunday afternoon. She was wrung out—first from wondering if Hal wanted to get back together, then from celebrating when he did. Saturday she slept and did narcissistic things like plucking her eyebrows and examining enlarged pores and doing her nails. Restful, absorbing, repetitious things.

Sundays at Cloud Peaks were much like other days for the staff. Karen was busy. After lunch Barb bundled up dirty clothes and was on her way to the washhouse when Kelly called her to the phone. Kelly and Tony were an item and Barb was glad that had worked out.

"Ms. Door? This is Dr. Elton Hockaday at Memorial Hospital of Sheridan County."

"What's wrong?" Barb got a sick, cold feeling in the pit of her stomach.

"Hal Simmons asked me to call you. He got kicked by a horse at the fairgrounds today."

"How bad is it?" She couldn't breathe.

"We're waiting for X rays."

"Where was he kicked?"

"Left thigh. He wants out of the hospital, but he can't drive or even walk right now. If the bone's broken, it'll have to be set and he sure won't be able to walk then."

Barb had to clear her throat before she could ask, "Anything else?"

"He hit his head when he fell. Might have a mild concussion. We'd like to keep him overnight, but he doesn't have insurance and says he won't stay."

"I'll be right there. It'll take about an hour."

"We'll try to keep him here."

She found Karen and told her where she was going.

"This doesn't usually happen to warm cowboys. What are you going to do?" Karen asked.

"I don't know. Hal needs help and he asked for me."

"I thought the two of you were going to take it easy."

"What am I supposed to do? He can't even drive."

"You're setting yourself up."

"For what?"

"Some bad feelings down the line."

"I'll worry about that later."

"I know you're concerned about him," said Karen. "You're glad to get back with him, but you just got out of one situation, with Grimaldi, and now you're looking for the same thing. Where you're, I don't know, a doormat."

"That's my decision," said Barb tightly.

"I know, I know. I just think you're blowing it."

"Blowing what?"

"Wyoming. This chance to do something new."

"Then why does it feel right?"

"Because it's familiar. I don't know exactly what you're doing, but you won't get what you want."

"If I ever figure out what that is. At least I'm being a good friend in the meantime."

Karen shrugged, gave Barb a hug, and a whispered, "Good luck. You're hopeless."

Barb drove down the mountain, and never had the trip to the blacktop taken so long. She knew speeding was stupid, but she risked it on the interstate and hoped the state cops weren't out this Sunday.

Please God, don't let it be bad, she said to herself. It *was* bad-serious or he wouldn't be in the hospital, but she hoped it wasn't serious-serious. If it were serious-serious, they wouldn't talk about letting him go home. But it can hurt like hell and not be terminal, like a migraine headache is a ten, but you never die from one. She didn't want him to feel bad, be sick. She didn't want for it to be terrible, for it to be permanent and painful and awful. Please God, she prayed, don't let it be awful.

DeSmet Lake lay serene and bare, deep blue and glassy in the sun. It was a surprising lake. There were no creeks feeding it, no trees, no underbrush growing close to the water, no exposed tree roots tangled at the banks, no bushes drooping branches in the water. Unlike lakes in the Midwest it was just bare, sage-dotted hills to the water's edge. Pickup conversions and RVs clustered around the boat ramps. It lay calm as a sapphire in its plain setting. Water is precious in Wyoming and the sight of so much all at once was like a mirage. Maybe Wyoming was a mirage—something unexpected, not quite real, beauty to wonder about, pain to fear.

Just thinking about the hospital brought back the smell of tape and disinfectant and ethyl alcohol.

It was just a cyst and the gynecologist didn't think it was serious, but she had to go in every month to be checked and it didn't get any bigger, but it didn't go away, either. She lived with fear, swinging from "This isn't happening to me" to "I am a dead woman." She would wake up every morning and have a few seconds of peace before she remembered, then the fear gripped and she had to fight panic. She wouldn't give in and let it rule her. After all, it probably wasn't serious, nothing to get upset over.

Finally the gynecologist said, "Let's get it out of there." And she had a date to go to the hospital and she packed a bag and found substitutes to teach her classes and tried to read up on it, as though knowing what was going to happen was a defense. In the morning they prepped her and put her to sleep, and when she woke up she felt worse than she'd ever felt until they gave her a shot of something.

The next time she woke up she was in her room and Marty was sitting beside the bed. He was hollow-eyed and looked worried.

"You don't need to stay here," Barb said. It was hard to talk because her mouth was dry. "I'm just going to sleep."

"How are you?" he asked.

"Rotten, but I'll be okay."

And the next time she woke up, late that night, he was still there, looking haunted and needing a shave.

"You ought to go home," she said. "It must be boring to watch me sleep."

"I want to make sure you can ask for help if you need it."

So she turned to get the call button, and when she rolled onto her side she groaned and he rose up out of the chair. Everything hurt when she tried to move. She knew she'd have to move sooner or later, but she wanted to move as little as possible just then. She shifted on her back until she could grasp the button, then put it where she could reach it easily.

"I can manage," she said. "Go home and get some sleep."

So he left, and she was touched that he cared that much. It made her feel warm and loved and she thought Marty was wonderful to do that.

So driving to Sheridan on a bright, sunny Sunday, she remembered hurting and hoped it wouldn't be bad for Hal. And she could remember that Marty had loved her and he wasn't always or only a scuzzbucket.

20

Barb took the Fifth Street exit and gunned her car up the hill to the Sheridan hospital. It was a new brick building, neat and calm, surrounded by watered grass and parking lots. She hurried inside the emergency-room entrance, where she found the polished efficiency of people in uniforms going about their business.

"I'm looking for Dr. Hockaday," she told a nurse who looked up as she entered.

The nurse directed Barb to the other end of the room and she found a beefy man in greens who pointed toward a yellow-curtained cubicle.

"Hal?" She pulled the curtain back.

He lay propped, half sitting. They'd cut his jeans off and the sheet he clutched tightly to his waist didn't quite cover a removable cast. His belt and his shirt, dusty and blood-smeared, lay on top of his hat. He looked pale and uncomfortable.

Barb reached for his hand. She wanted to throw her arms around him, but didn't want to hurt him.

"How do you feel?"

"Like shit. Thanks for coming." They must have given him some painkiller because he had to stop and swallow before he could say more. "They won't let me go."

"Let's find out what's wrong before we talk about leaving."

"I'm *not* staying here."

"You're not leaving till the X rays are done. Your leg might be broken."

"Swell."

No sweet acceptance, no docile long-suffering. At least he was human.

She kissed him softly on the forehead, which was sweaty even in the air-conditioned room, and went to Elton Hockaday.

"Are the X rays back?"

"Yes." Hockaday looked like an ex-wrestler, with a starched lab coat unbuttoned over a bulging knit shirt. He stuck the film in a lighted frame. "No break."

Barb stared at the shadows on the film. She guessed it was good public relations to show people the film, but she never could make the shadows mean anything.

"He needs to stay off his feet. These cowboys think they're so tough they don't need time to heal."

"What can I do?" She knew she was going to be sorry as soon as she said it.

"Keep him in bed as long as you can." Hockaday turned and tore a printed sheet of instructions off a pad. "Follow this tonight, to make sure he doesn't have a concussion. If his head is as hard as his femur, he'll be okay, but someone needs to watch him."

The page fluttered in her shaking hand and she quickly folded it and stuffed it in her handbag.

"Can I take him home?"

"I guess so. I'd like to keep him overnight, but as I said, he wants O-U-T."

"I don't have any insurance," Hal said as they prepared to leave.

"Do you have your checkbook?" Barb asked.

"No."

"I'll take care of it and we can settle up later."

"Just tell them to bill me. Stay out of it."

"I'm already in it and I'm trying to be patient because I know you feel bad, but there's no need to be mean."

"Tell them."

Accounting would not agree to bill him, so she wrote a check on her Kansas City bank, which they accepted. It didn't make sense, but they couldn't phone his local bank on a Sunday. They wanted Hal's address and Karen's in Buffalo and at Cloud Peaks. Barb got a pair of her jeans from the car because, as usual, Hal wasn't wearing underwear, and he wouldn't leave the ER wrapped in a sheet. Her jeans didn't fit, but they covered the territory.

It seemed to take the day to drive back to Story and get him into bed. She helped him wash and got him a clean T-shirt. She heard his teeth grind when she pulled the jeans off. After a long search she found some boxer shorts in a bottom drawer. She insisted he put the Velcro-fastened nylon cast back on. And she brought him a Ziplok ice bag.

She fixed him some soup and sandwiches and noted the time until his next codeine pill. Then she pulled the rocking chair up to his bed.

"Look what you've gotten us into this time, Ollie," she said.

He smiled a little. "This wasn't what I had in mind." He tried to shift in bed and she saw his face change before he caught himself.

"I'll get some groceries tomorrow and wash those clothes. Where's your dirty-clothes hamper?"

"It's a box on the closet floor. Get some beer when you're out."

"I'll check. I don't know if you can drink beer and take codeine."

"Get it anyway."

She pulled the box out and sorted their dirty clothes together. "I need a flashlight, too."

"What for?"

"I'm supposed to check the pupils of your eyes every hour tonight."

"It's in the pickup."

It took a second, then they both remembered they didn't have the pickup.

"It's at the fairgrounds," he said.

"Is it safe there?"

"Safe enough. If somebody doesn't drive it here, I'll phone the Ketchams and ask Garey to move it over by their house. He's the manager and they live on the grounds."

"What'll I use for a flashlight?" she asked, studying the concussion sheet.

"Just turn the shitting light on."

"Right, Captain. Beam me up, Scottie. Hostile life-forms down here."

"What are you doing?!" Barb shrieked.

"Taking a shower," Hal said the next morning. He lifted his bad leg out of the bed and swung the other over.

"Can't you just take a sponge bath in bed? That's what they do in hospitals. You could fall."

"I'm gritty from working yesterday."

Hal took his cane and Barb stepped around to open the bathroom door. He almost lost his balance and grabbed the counter beside the sink.

"Let me help you." She peeled his T-shirt off and pulled down his boxers.

"Get this fucking thing off."

She knelt and unpeeled the Velcro of his cast. She gasped when she saw the perfect horseshoe of mangled flesh on his thigh. The swollen leg was bruised black around the horseshoe, and raw meat seeped around the scabs.

"Oh my God."

"Son of a bitch," he said when he tried to put weight on the bad leg to get the good one over the bottom edge of the shower.

She tried not to look. She felt so bad she was almost sick. Pity flooded her.

"Stay here," he demanded.

She stood by the shower and he balanced on one leg and quickly soaped himself. She held the shower curtain open in case he fell. Water splashed all over her, all over the floor. He swore again when he couldn't reach his bad leg, so she carefully ran the soapy cloth down his thigh. He hissed through his teeth. She braced herself against the side of the little shower and said, "Lean on me." Hal pivoted to rinse his back, then put a heavy arm over her shoulders and she took his weight as he stepped out.

"Hold on to the wall and take the cane," she said. She toweled him off, then pushed the bath mat out of his way with her foot. He almost pulled her off balance. They edged to the bed where he sat heavily.

"Son of a bitch."

He pulled on the clean T-shirt she handed him and she helped get the boxers up. Then he twisted around, piled up the pillows, and edged back into the bed. She lifted his bad leg.

She went to the bathroom for the cast, which had gotten splashed. He took it, but didn't put it on. She got deodorant and his comb from the bathroom.

He was examining the meat loaf when she returned. She could see how much his left leg was swollen compared with his good leg. Tears overflowed and she felt she didn't have a right to cry.

"It's all right, Barb," he said. He looked up at her and smiled. "I've been stove up worse."

"Sorry. I just can't . . ." She felt dizzy and dropped into the rocker.

"Put your head between your knees," he said. After a few minutes she sat up.

"Sorry. I never do that."

"I didn't know it would upset you."

"Now, don't *you* apologize."

"This is the first crack I've seen in your image," he mused.

"What image?"

"Cool, controlled Madame Professor."

"I wasn't very controlled in bed."

"That's different. This is warmth, not heat."

"I'm going to spackle the image closed," she said.

"It's okay to feel bad when someone gets hurt," he said. His eyes were gentle and it was like the time he said it was okay to be stupid. She pulled the chair up close and took his hand, but she cried and had to drop it to wipe and blow.

"That's what I like about you," he whispered. "You're so intense. In bed, I know you're only thinking about what we're doing. When you want to learn something, you go at it like a dog on a bone. All out. And when you see my leg, you're hurting with me."

She knelt beside him and he put his hand on her hair, like a blessing.

Later, he got up and limped into the kitchen to eat, then watched TV for a while. The next morning was a little better, but he insisted on going into the office to make phone calls and there was no place but a desk drawer to prop his foot and he could barely walk when he finished. He quit taking the Tylenol with codeine and got up more and the pain made him cranky. Barb was getting edgy, so she went out to do laundry and get groceries.

She wanted to drive to Cloud Peaks and pull the covers over her head. Hal wasn't supposed to get hurt. He was supposed to be strong. She resented having to stay locked up with him. It wasn't the scutwork and she knew it. It was worrying and feeling bad. It was knowing she couldn't do anything about how bad he felt or how long he would take to heal.

He wouldn't leave the cast on and he wouldn't stay off the leg. He prowled the trailer like a bad-tempered lion. She tried to remember that pain tired you out and that he couldn't help being grouchy, but she didn't know how long she could play Florence Nightingale.

21

Hal caught up on paperwork. Money trickled in from the ranches. While he was going through the mail on Wednesday he said, "What really chaps me is that slob, Curry, is making bucks taking my place." Hal had just talked to a client he couldn't service. "Curry's got the highest AQ in the county."

"AQ?" asked Barb.

"Asshole Quotient."

She laughed, then said, "Somebody has to do it. Horses don't wait."

"He knows how to shoe, but he's not careful. If he does a bad job, it won't show up at first. Then I'll have to go back and try to fix what he messed up."

"So? Everyone will recognize your value."

"No, I'll get blamed, too."

"You make good money shoeing."

"When I work. I don't make anything laying around here."

"It's hard work. You go out too soon, you'll collapse trying to do too much."

"I never fall out."

"Right. John Wayne never faints."

"That's a cheap shot! I can take care of myself." He stood up and leaned over the desk. "You can cash in your martyr points for a prize and leave."

"You ungrateful son of a bitch."

"I'm not ungrateful. It's just getting on my nerves having you here."

"Having me see you when you aren't strong and healthy."

Then he pounded the desktop so hard she jumped. The papers bounced. His face flushed and his hands clenched. "I hate it when I can't be up and around. And working. And it was my own fault. The last time I shoed that horse, he almost got me. I was tired from working late Saturday, and I miscalculated and he kicked me. Damn."

Hal grabbed the cane, stumped into the living room, and let himself down into the couch. "I hate it when I see how shaky this is—shoeing horses, no security except the CDs at United Savings. I should go to Denver, find a real job. Work in an office. Medical insurance, all the benefits."

"Why don't you?"

He didn't say anything.

Barb knew why he didn't leave—his little girl in Casper. She'd seen the camaraderie with his friends. She'd been there long enough to love the hills and canyons and lakes and mountains, the blue Big Horns where the sun went each night. She couldn't imagine Hal breathing stale air-conditioning and taking orders from a pale, soft-handed manager. She tried to put him in a three-piece suit looking out of a skyscraper window. He would see the mountains west of Denver and wish, always, he were out there.

"When I can't work, I think too much," he said. "I see cobwebs on the ceiling I never noticed. I hate having to ask you for everything. I have time to think about my life. How I'm going nowhere and besides feeling crappy, it's depressing, all right?"

She sat beside him and tried to hug him, but he shrugged her off. She sat with her hands in her lap, feeling helpless. His outdoor tan had faded a little and gray smudged under his eyes.

"This reminds me of all the other times I've been laid up," he said. "Every time it takes longer to heal. I feel bad and I don't care what happens in the world. That's what dying must be like—you feel bad and you don't care." He stared at the wall, not seeing anything. Then he said, "Oh, hell."

She pulled him into her arms and held him for a long time.

After he got through the bills, he spent hours in the office with his foot propped on the upended wastebasket, the keyboard of his computer in his lap. He was learning how to write programs, with the idea of phasing into that business. There was very little work shoeing in the winter. A friend of his went to Arizona and rounded up wild cattle on the border, then came back to Buffalo County for branding, when it was time to take the cows to summer pasture.

The next morning she watched Hal eat scrambled eggs and toast.

"Do you like the eggs?" She looked at his face to see what he'd say.

"They're fine."

"You didn't like them."

"Hey, it's not that important. The eggs were okay, and anyway, you don't have to please me all the time."

"I'm just trying to take care of you."

"I appreciate that. But ever since you saw my leg and cracked the facade, you've been bitchy."

"Me bitchy? You're so cranky I want to send you to your room."

"I've never seen anybody so walled up," he said.

"Maybe I'm careful. If you'd been through what I went through, you'd be prickly, too."

"You told me part of it at Clearmont. Tell me the rest."

"I'll go to pieces." She put her coffee cup down. She was spilling it on her jeans.

"Go to pieces. Maybe you'll feel better," he said.

She looked at the yellow streaks and toast crumbs on her plate. "Then you'll think I'm stupid and self-pitying."

"Come here."

They walked over to the couch and he sat with his leg propped on the coffee table. He spread one arm to welcome her.

"You are stupid and self-pitying."

"Thanks." She sat and thought for a few minutes. Maybe he was right. Maybe she could get rid of some of the bad feelings. "Everything I counted on was gone. He didn't leave me earlier because he never found anybody better. I thought we were good for each other but he was just marking time because nothing better came along!"

"Easy, easy."

"That was the meanest thing he could say. I thought we were partners, friends, lovers. We came together like two halves of a coin, a perfect fit. Not perfect, maybe, but damn good. I thought he was the only person who ever came close to loving me like my dad loved me—just because I was me."

Hal held her. "Easy, baby, easy. I'm here," he said. He wasn't going to leave or punish her or withdraw because she was dumb and self-pitying and crazy.

It felt good to drain some of the hurt, like lancing an infection.

"Marty couldn't stand me like this. He was cool and this embarrassed him. He was too cool about everything. He never let me love him enough and I couldn't let myself go, the way I do with you."

"He probably couldn't handle it if you were crazy-wild," said Hal.

"No. He froze up."

"As long as you were insecure and proper, you depended on him."

"Oh, hell, was that it?"

"And you're intense."

"All my life people have been telling me I shouldn't feel what I feel. Or I shouldn't feel it so strongly."

"It's hard to handle."

"I know." She brushed the edges of his mustache with the back of her finger, then touched his lips. His upper lip was thin, obscured by the mustache, but the lower lip was full and soft. "I'm glad it doesn't scare you off."

He stroked her hair. "It sounds like a rough few months. Enough to make you closed."

"I hurt so much after it happened, I made myself sick. I don't want to feel that bad."

"How does this feel?"

"All right." She was surprised. "It feels all right."

She went to the kitchen to wash dishes and wondered how long it would hurt and how long it would take before the pain no longer surprised her. She always thought she faced the truth and handled what came along, then some hidden emotion she had denied would rise up and smite her and she was always shocked at its power. She hated not being aware of her own routines or hidden agendas.

When she finished the dishes, she said, "We're going for a drive."

"What for?"

"I need to get out of here. Cabin fever."

"You don't know what cabin fever is. Stay here in the winter and see what it's really like."

"C'mon."

He wanted to take the cast off, but Barb was adamant. He grumbled as he eased himself onto her car seat and lifted his leg inside. "There's more room in the pickup."

"I'm used to this car." She unfolded a map and he said, "No, I'll tell you," and directed her to a red gravel state road. She wasn't sure where they were going, but at least they were out in the fresh air and sunshine. They passed DeSmet Lake and came out on the road to Ucross.

The rows of spume from the irrigator sprinklers rose like feathers from the serpent god's brow—a new fertility rite of water. Geysers arched from the aluminum pipes, portable fountains on wheels. Some were siderolls, where the pipe, acting as the axle for big, spoked wheels, spanned the field, each spray ticking its circle like a yard sprinkler. Some were center pivots, spraying huge circles of earth green, making the brown hills seem drier and more rugged next to the lush, damp alfalfa. Ranchers irrigated, if they had the water, to grow hay for winter feeding, to grow more cattle, make more money. But they also made the valley beautiful and the late-afternoon sun caught rainbows in the spray.

Just before the junkyard they saw twenty wild turkeys in a row on the fence. He directed her to Triple Creek Park. He waved to a thin young man with an innocent smile who rode a mower over the grass around the barn. Barb parked at the farmhouse.

"Is this too far for you to walk?"

Hal shook his head. He limped across the thick, watered grass, then down the wooden steps, across the creek bottoms, then to a picnic table outside the shelter. He seemed to soak up the dry air, the bright sunlight, the green tree shadows, and the rush of the creeks. He turned, sniffing like a dog, and absorbed the rust hills and the sage clumps, the cattle pastured nearby, the smell of the cut grass by the farmhouse. She left him alone and walked to where two creeks met. Scruffy box elder and willows grew along the creeks and she liked them because they weren't landscaped. She picked up a couple of river-scoured stones for paperweights, rubbed mud off them with her thumb. She could smell mint and watercress upstream. She joined him at a picnic table.

"Tell me why you fell in love with this Marty in the first place."

"I don't want to get into it."

"You need to."

She took a deep breath. She squeezed her stones. She couldn't talk. She knew what resistance felt like and this was stronger. She felt as though Hal were telling her to do more than she could manage. She wasn't afraid of losing her composure or looking awful. She was afraid she would go mad. At the same time she knew that the thing she was most afraid of was the thing she most needed to do.

"I can't recall the sequence exactly," she began. "I was back in town after finishing my degree and working in New York. I came back to help Mom. I was feeling out the local colleges in case I had to stay awhile. Daddy was in and out of the hospital by then, and Cindy had kids and I was the one who could drive him to chemotherapy and make sure Mom remembered to eat and keep things going at home.

"I don't remember exactly, but around that time I was offered a good position at the university. And Dad died."

It had been seven years, but thinking about her dad still made her feel shaky.

"You liked your dad?" Hal sat on the picnic table with his left leg stretched out and Barb sat on the bench between his legs, facing away as he rubbed her shoulders. She could hear his soft voice and feel him surrounding her.

"Sure. He was Daddy. He thought I was adorable. He thought I was smart and pretty and wonderful and he never criticized or nagged like Mom. I was perfect enough the way I was." *Look at me, Daddy! See how pretty I am. Watch me dance. Isn't this a becoming dress? I put it on just for you.* "When he died, I felt like there was no one left in the world who loved me without conditions. I mean, I knew my mother and sister loved me, but it was never that unrestrained, uncritical, accepting love."

"Sometimes I think we spend the rest of our lives trying for that," said Hal. "So then what happened?"

"I went to work at the university, maybe that was before Daddy died, it's hard to remember what happened when. And right after that I met Marty when he joined the department. He was friendly and funny and intelligent. We met at a faculty party and he asked me out right away and then we wanted to make love on the first date. 'This isn't just a one-night thing, Barb,' he said. When I looked in his eyes, it was that other-half-of-the-coin match. I felt complete. It was a big scandal back then when he moved in with me, but we didn't care. I was a dry sponge that filled up. At first, he did little things that made me melt. He'd go to the bakery for French bread, then cook onion soup from scratch. Browned the onions, added the stock, grated the Swiss cheese for the top. He brought me coffee in bed in the morning. He bought cut flowers in the winter. He cared about my classes, my writing, and he didn't compete. He came and got me for sunsets." Barb started crying softly. Hal rubbed her shoulders.

"When I was in the hospital, he was so worried he just came and sat, even when I was zonked on Demerol. He loved me." She just sat there with tears running down her face. She missed her dad and she missed Marty and all the good stuff came back. She thought of all the things she and Marty had together and loved together.

She could see the thin grass under the table and hear the shush of the cottonwood leaves as they flickered shadows at her feet. Then she reached for Hal. He wrapped her in his arms. The sadness was drowning her. She wouldn't go mad, she would just weep forever and not be able to stop. Somewhere, when she least expected it, her defenses would slip for a second and all the overwhelming loneliness and insecurity would drown her. Say the right word and the crazy lady would cry because there was more grief inside than she could hold.

"I'm going to kick a cripple," said Hal, his face buried in her hair. She could feel his breath on her ear.

"What?" She rubbed her face with a sleeve.

"I feel like I'm kicking you when you're down, but now is the time. When you can hear it."

"I can't bear any more."

"Yes," he said, and squeezed her harder. "What was it like, being the other half of the coin?"

"What do you mean?"

"It must have been a good feeling, when you fell in love with Marty. You felt complete. And when he left, you tried to find another match."

"What do you mean?" She tightened up.

"What have you been doing since you came to Wyoming? With me and the other men?"

"You mean I was trying." She made herself say it. "To feel complete? Oh, hell. Am I that dumb?"

"Realize what you've been doing."

"I've been trying to find the other half. That's what I was doing with Curry and Mac. Oh, God. And with you." She got up from the picnic table. She had no right to the comfort of his arms. "Is that what I've been doing?" She was embarrassed, as though she'd been walking around naked without knowing it. Everyone else had noticed but her. "I thought I was hot stuff—professional woman, good credentials, a mortgage."

"And you're playing housekeeper and nursemaid and caretaker, trying to fit yourself to me." Hal stayed on the picnic table while she paced in front.

"Oh, God. I was going to ask you to come back to Kansas City. I had it all worked out. Lots of high-tech jobs, United Telecom, Sprint. All the agribusiness, Farmland. You could find a job with some security so you'd know where you were going. And I'd have you to make me feel complete." She stopped. "I was using you!"

"Take it easy. I'm glad you wanted me to be with you, but you see what you're doing?"

"Looking for the other half. Damn."

"And now you see it's bullshit. If I said no, you'd want to move here." She cringed. She had thought of that.

"You mold yourself to a man, like the slip on a clay pot, then you resent it, do something to break off the relationship."

"Oh, God." And all of it fell into place. That was why buying the hat bothered her. Why she couldn't follow through with Curry. She tried to collect bad feelings over that morning's scrambled eggs. A headache exploded and the pain tried to get out. She rubbed her temple, but that made it worse.

"I feel bloodsucked," said Hal in a low voice. "Like you're clawing for pieces of me." He was almost apologetic. He knew this was hard to take. And that she wouldn't like him for doing it, at least not very soon. It had taken a lot of strength for him to say these things. And affection—you don't bother with someone you don't care about.

"That's the last thing I wanted to do," she cried. She hated him and loved him for pushing her so she realized what she was doing. She wanted to escape. She couldn't stand the humiliation. She wanted to get away from him, because she was chagrined that he had seen through her routines when she couldn't.

"You're driving with the brakes on." He got down off the table and walked over to her. He took her in his arms. She tried to pull away, but he wouldn't release her. She was afraid she'd hurt his bad leg if she struggled. He pinned her arms in a bear hug.

"I need to think about this," she said. "I've got to get out of here." She was desperate. She couldn't just stand there and pretend she didn't feel stupid and embarrassed and exposed.

He kissed her cheek, brushed her hair away from her neck. His mouth was close to her ear and he whispered, "Take some time out." Then he released her.

They drove back to Story without talking. He popped a beer and watched her dump her things in her tote. He stood at the door with his weight on his good leg. Barb felt the cold shiver when she thought of his bad leg. He held the doorjamb with one hand and pulled her into a hug with the other.

"I'm leaving." She sounded desperate. She was shaking apart inside.

He gave her a thoughtful kiss.

22

Barb headed back to Cloud Peaks. She felt spread-eagle naked on the biggest billboard in town. She wanted to leave Cloud Peaks, leave the Big Horns and go where she didn't feel stupid and revealed.

Later that day she talked to Karen about what had happened with Hal.

"For an otherwise intelligent person, you can be awfully dense," Karen repeated. She smiled as though Barb were a slow but well-loved student. It was that quiet time in late afternoon when the main room of the lodge was deserted while the cook and the girls got dinner ready and the guests were in their cabins. Smells of homemade bread and roasting beef floated in from the kitchen. Voices mingled with the sound of china as the girls set the table. The sun was still high in the sky, but the angle had changed and the day had taken a pause.

"What am I supposed to do? Stop feeling? Stop wanting?" Barb asked.

"I don't think anybody can do that. But I kind of see what Hal means. You came back from the depression and being with men was part of the cure."

"It felt good."

"Of course."

"I'm supposed to tell Marty good-bye, kiss off seven years, and instantly achieve some sort of autonomy I didn't know I lacked and everything's fine?" Barb had trouble keeping her voice down.

"Well, of course it's not that easy." Karen stood with the box of Christmas presents at the front desk of the lodge. It was almost hot, even at eight thousand feet. High July.

"It might help to get away. Why don't you go up to the pack camp with the next group of guests?"

"On a horse? No, thanks."

"Well, there's Thermopolis and Jackson and Yellowstone. It would be a shame to come all this way and not see Yellowstone. Have you ever been there?"

"Not since I was a kid."

"There's no place like it. It's jammed with tourists, of course, but it's still special."

Karen lifted the box and headed toward the kitchen storerooms. Barb drifted back to the cabin and flopped on her bed. All this outdoors stuff scared her. She didn't want to go off alone and look at geysers and mountains. She could do that on PBS. Maybe she did need to spend some time by herself. Alone, not with guests. That afternoon, she asked Karen about camping.

"You changed your mind?" Karen asked, surprised.

"I don't have any equipment," said Barb.

"We've got everything. Are you sure?"

"No. Being completely on my own is what I need to do. I'm afraid to camp, so camping is what I need to do."

"Brave words, Kimosabe."

"Well, yes, I might not be doing the right thing, but let's try it and see what happens. You can laugh at me if I can't manage."

Face it, Princess. Looking for a warm cowboy had felt good, but had been the wrong thing to do.

This felt strange, but she had a hunch this was the right thing to do. At first she scared herself with her usual anticamping routine—lions and tigers and bears, oh my. Or more likely, elk and rattlesnakes and mountain lions. Then she began to feel curious. How would she react, out alone in the woods? What would she do if some animal came along? She had to find out.

The next morning Sully, a grinning kid from the University of Colorado, led her up to about ten thousand feet. The grass got sparser in the brown, sandy soil, small ferns grew beside the path, and even the sage shrank to a smaller-leafed plant on a tough, woody stem. Where the tall, scaly-bark pines thinned, ground cover of tiny, tear-shaped leaves flourished and hidden birds called. They rode guests' horses and Sully had loaded everything for a three-day camp-out on a packhorse. Sully took her to an old hunting campsite and unloaded and put up the tent and helped her carry the bags inside and teased her about moose and buffalo.

"Buffalo? C'mon," she said. "Even dude ladies know there aren't any free-ranging buffalo around here."

Sully grinned devilishly. "Well, maybe not buffalo, but elk and deer, and raccoons and smaller animals."

"What's in these packs?"

"Don't you know?" He sounded amazed.

"No. I don't do this. Camping, I mean. I asked Karen to put it together."

"Well, this is food, and keep it locked up. Bears like most things people eat."

"Bears!"

"Not very likely." He loosened a rope and said, "I'll put this wood out by the campfire ring. There's a hatchet in the bottom, in case you run out and need more. This pack is the sleeping bag, ground cloth, and pad. This one is pots and pans and what you need to cook. I hope you brought your own clothes and things."

"Yes, I've got that stuff."

"Well, that does it, then." He stood, hands on hips, and surveyed the campsite, checking off his own mental list. She hoped Karen had covered the essentials.

"You sure you'll be okay by yourself?" he asked. "I can't remember anybody wanting to be all by herself."

"I'll be fine, and if I'm not, I'll walk back."

"Okay. Just watch out for grizzlies." Sully grinned and left.

The mountains frightened her. Snakes. Getting

lost. Falling. If she hurt herself, so she couldn't walk, it would be a long time before anyone found her. If they found her.

Some geological contraction a million years in the past pushed the mountains up from the seafloor, tilted them into the sky. Time clothed them with trees and grass, then the animals came. They were too much to take on alone.

It was noon and she had the rest of the day to fill.

Except for the break for the path, the clearing was surrounded by evergreens, mostly yellow pine with straggly limbs and irregular, plated bark. The stiff needles fanned at the ends of twigs. Currant bushes underneath drew birds to feed. Thin mountain grass carpeted the clearing and a small, swift creek ran around the west edge.

The loneliness was overwhelming. Her heart hammered and she forced herself to sit calmly, her back to a black boulder, and breathe. She could find her way back. She didn't have to stay here. She could be home in time for tea. She could imagine the wranglers' teasing if she came back early.

Birds called their territorial notices. Wind whispered through the hundred-foot evergreens. That clean pine smell feathered by her on the wind. A squirrel hurried past on his errands. The sun found gaps through the trees. Her heart slowed and breathing became regular.

Not ten feet away grew a cluster of the blue bell flowers she had seen on her ride with Tony. They nodded, heavy-headed, the bottom blossoms shriveled purple. She crawled over, her knees and hands kneading the soft ground, and crouched before them. She bent and sniffed. A faint herbal scent. She couldn't get close enough, so she lay flat and looked up inside the cup of the blossoms. Then she stuck her nose right up to the thimbles of petals and sniffed. A faint, but unmistakable smell. From underneath she could see backlighted veins in the blue petals. Each blossom hung on a curve of needle-fine stem arching from the main stalk. The moist earth cracked where the stalk emerged and three more plants clustered within a hand's span. The bell darkened where the stamen emerged bearing furry yellow pollen at the tip. A few grains dusted the sides of the bell, loosened from the filament.

She touched the five-point bell, stroked its curve with her little finger, studied the line of the curve, repeated for each blossom. The flower shriveled almost as she touched it, like the wilting blossoms near the bottom of the stalk, the first ones blown, which collapsed in minute violet wrinkles, shrunken inside their green receptacles.

She pulled off one blue corolla, and touched the yellow heart with her tongue. Did she taste the nectar? She eased around the plant to see it from another angle and the bell's curves repeated in the needle stem and the arching stalk. There were the other bellflowers growing with the other spaced and frugal plants the soil supported. She stood up and looked down on the blue cluster. The color blended with the soil and she could scarcely tell where the serrated edges of the petals stopped and the dark, damp ground began. Then she lay on her side with her head on her outstretched arm and stared at the flowers, just stared at them.

The flower was more real than she. She was disembodied and listless. She would look up this flower in the reference book in the lodge, but naming it wouldn't make any difference. It knew who it was. She would learn.

After lunch she walked to the creek, then made a timid foray into the woods, found a path, and walked away from the clearing. The path ended at a cliff and she almost walked off the mountain, grabbed a sticky cedar, and looked out over the canyon. Water crashed over the falls and rose in misty spray. It was like the gorge at Cloud Peaks, magnified. More beautiful, more breathtaking. She wanted to fly.

She crouched down, still holding the little tree, and tried to take it all in. Cloud shadows dimmed the canyon, then a shaft of piercing light shone through a break in the clouds. A place on the opposite wall of the canyon stood out, gilded and brilliant. She was beauty-blitzed.

She wanted to float out over the canyon, swoop and dart like some intoxicated raptor. She wanted to float to the bottom and follow the river, skim the rapids, land in a tree clinging to the side of the canyon, stroke upward, circle the river, float through the spume of the falls.

The sun had moved across the sky a few degrees as she stood there, and the light changed. Clouds darkened the canyon and the air seemed colder, then the wind picked up and flattened her jacket to her ribs. She looked into the rushing, foaming water and felt the power—endless water racing off the edge of the falls. She wondered where, up higher, the water began and how far it had traveled and how much farther it had to go. She was inside the water. She was inside the wet and the rush and the strength. She ran over rocky beds and twisted through meadows, carried stones, felt fish flicker past, then gathered strength and rushed to the falls, hurled herself over the edge, and exploded into foam, into mist, into wind, into sun. She spread into curving light, hung suspended in the air, fell and rejoined her body, raced to the next falls, flew into the bottom of the canyon, burst into foaming billows.

Wind breathed spray on her face and she was the water. It was on her and in her and she was the water. She was the air and the light. She was the earth that held the water, the creases and fissures in the canyon's sides. She was the trees and the rocks and the animals that lived there and the soil that slowly formed. She lived in the sun and she was the earth and its heart throbbed in her.

Light moved, shadows shifted. Rain peppered down. Mist rose from the caldron at the bottom of the falls. Double rainbows floated across the canyon walls. A raven wheeled over the river, then dived for invisible prey. The mist and the wind touched her, then the sun faltered behind clouds.

Back at her campsite, she made dinner, then watched the stars come out and had no more thoughts than a stone. She sat hugging her knees and stared into the flames until they burned down. She got in the tent and crawled into the sleeping bag, but didn't sleep. The ground was hard even with the foam pad. In the dark every noise threatened. A night bird called and she jerked up. She felt the tent closing in, but didn't want to leave it because the mountain wind blew steady and cold outside. And if she left the tent, she'd have nothing between her and lions and tigers and bears.

She knew it was absurd. She was outdoors, there was plenty of air. But her chest felt squeezed and she kept taking deep breaths. She couldn't fill her lungs. She tried blowing out the air, pushing it all out, then breathing, but she couldn't get enough. She flailed out of the sleeping bag and grabbed her coat and stuck her feet in her shoes and pushed the tent flap open. Once outside, she heard rustling and crackling in the woods around the campsite. She held her breath. Were there footfalls? She couldn't get enough air. Had she come just enough higher up the mountain to pass some oxygen limit? She started another small fire by the light from the lantern.

She scanned the dark outside the campfire's light circle, but saw no animal eyes like orange reflectors, looking back.

After a while she calmed down and went back to the tent and started to get in the sleeping bag again and couldn't breathe. Panic breaths, fast shallow breaths. *In*hale. *In*hale. The mountain was tipping over to bury her. She grabbed her shoes and the sleeping bag and scrambled out of the tent. Maybe she could run back down the path ahead of the avalanche. She stood in the big clearing, barefoot, and listened for the rumble of the falling rocks.

Silence. She put her shoes on, listened some more. Wind in the trees made the branches creak and the needles sigh. She jumped at an owl's hoot.

Then quiet. She put another piece of wood on the coals, waited. She could breathe again.

She felt silly. There was no avalanche. The tent was not coming down on top of her. There was enough air here for anybody. But she knew she couldn't breathe if she went in the tent again and that it would close in on her.

She dragged her sleeping bag and ground cloth and pad over to the fire and put a few sticks of firewood close to hand. She curled just outside the ring of stones and, sometime later, finally fell asleep.

The next day Barb wandered in the surrounding woods. Found what she thought were elk scats. Found tiny, tart raspberries. She picked dozens, scratching her hands and getting sticky with their juice. Built fires and ate her solitary meals. Trout lazed in a natural pool upstream from the clearing. They fitted the pool the way the sky fitted between the evergreen branches. She had thought there would be nothing to do, but found more than she had time to study.

The second evening she placed a blue feather and a stone that looked like a bone on a rock before the fire, spread her sleeping bag, and fell asleep as soon as her feet warmed up.

Thunder woke her and she watched lightning dance across the mountain. Then it began to rain. She gingerly dragged her things inside the tent. She lay down with her head at the open flap. She wasn't happy, but she couldn't sleep out in the rain. She heard the first drops hit the tent and the branches of the pines and the dry leaves and needles, then the rain was a steady patter. She was cold and the sleeping bag and her clothes felt dank. Mist dampened her face, and drops spattered when the wind changed. Her sleeping bag would get muddy and wet, but she didn't care. The next night she built a fire, ate, and spread her damp sleeping bag just outside the stone ring.

She came awake with heart pounding and didn't know where she was. Then she smelled the wood smoke from the red coals of the dying fire and saw the outline of the tent. What had awakened her? She unzipped the sleeping bag and sat up. Then she heard it again—an animal.

She thrashed around, tangled in her sleeping bag. Her heart catapulted to her throat and hammered there. "Son of a bitch. Damn." She struggled out of the sleeping bag and to her feet.

At the creek side of the clearing, a pair of orange eyes reflected the last of the campfire's light. She couldn't tell what it was. The eyes were too low for a deer or elk. Then the animal loped toward her, and as he neared the fire she saw a wolf's grinning muzzle, the pointed ears, the dainty feet. The wolf had just drunk at the creek, she thought. Water dripped from his mouth. Then she thought: rabies!

He kept coming and she panicked because that was wrong. A healthy animal in the wild avoids people, but a rabid one seeks them. She picked up a piece of firewood and threw it, but he didn't even bother to swerve to avoid it, her aim was so bad. All she had was her sleeping bag, still wrapped around one hand. When the wolf circled the fire, she flapped the sleeping bag at him. He jerked his

LOVE WITH A WARM COWBOY 221

head and snapped at it so fast she didn't see, but only heard his teeth rip the fabric.

"Please go away." The first time it came out a whisper. She swallowed and tried again. "Get out of here!" she screamed. "You don't want anything here."

The wolf pulled his muzzle out of the quilted nylon. Desperate and angry, she flapped it at him again, stamped her feet, and shouted, "Get away, get away."

He lunged at her. She flung the sleeping bag between them and he leaped and snapped again. The sleeping bag was only slowing him down. It wasn't going to scare him away or hurt him. He backed off and she bent to the stack of firewood. Without taking her eyes off the wolf, she grasped a stout log.

She stamped one foot and brandished the log. If she could hit him with it, he might leave. But it was only a foot long and he could lunge past it to her bare hand. He trotted back and forth, looking for a way through the sleeping bag. The fire was dying and it was harder to see him.

Then he feinted, lashed out, and leaped for her face. She threw the sleeping bag in front of her, and his teeth sank into the nylon inches from her cheek. Before he could recover, she bludgeoned him with the log.

He let out a brief, high-pitched yelp, fell away from the sleeping bag, and backed off. She couldn't see that she'd hurt him any, but he loped off into the darkness.

She sat shakily on the pad and stared at the flames. A rabid wolf? Unheard of in the Big Horns. And she'd scared it away! She still pumped too

much adrenaline to be calm. She felt powerful—
she had faced her fears, one of them.

After a while the flames hypnotized her and she slept.

23

The next morning Barb was cold and stiff, but she felt good. She would have expected to be shaky and nervous, but in daylight it all seemed matter-of-fact. And she was hungry.

She built up a fire and cooked most of a pound package of bacon, then scrambled the last four eggs. She tore open the rolls and thickly buttered them.

I could have been killed, or savaged, or infected with the rabies virus, she thought. But I wasn't. I survived claustrophobia and my fears and I defended myself against a real menace and won. My God, I won.

She stripped and walked to the creek. She liked the sun on her skin. At the creek she lay on her stomach, enjoyed the touch of the feathery grass on her legs. She stretched her arms out and pressed her cheek to the earth. The wind was cool, so she washed quickly and rotated layers of clothing, trying to get a fresh shirt next to her skin.

Later she walked in a new direction, through an unbroken expanse of trees, uphill. There was no path, but she knew she could find her way back. Hell, she could do anything. Something teased the edges of consciousness, something she wasn't seeing.

She felt strong and healthy and beautiful as she walked through the morning woods. Then she grasped the teasing idea. She had done this herself. Alone. She hadn't needed anyone else. She was the whole coin.

Barb sat, unfocused. She thought if she came camping, she would really get to know the mountain and she wouldn't be afraid. But what she learned was that she couldn't control it all. Not her fears, not the wolf, not the beauty of the waterfall.

She could never be in charge. Not of the flowers or the birds or the mountain. Or people. Not Grimaldi or Hal or even herself. Like trying to hold a rainbow. She was helpless. She felt a little breeze, and the sun, and smelled the earth. The wind was born up here.

It started in the lodgepole pines and picked up a few molecules of them, then the spruces and the alders and the flowers—the paintbrush and lupines—and the scats of the animals and their dander. Birdsongs—junkos and thrushes. Then the wind moved down the mountain to the reservoirs and creeks and the wood smoke from cabins. By the time it got to the foothills it carried pollen and dust. It picked up cottonwood fluff and alfalfa pollen from the hayfields. Then it blew across the valley and picked up weeds and sage and more dust and the spoor of cattle. More exhaust and people's effluvia. It was still thin and heady as wine as it blew over the rounded hills at Ucross.

And eastward.

She wanted to hold the wind and knew she couldn't. She couldn't hold any of it.

She stretched one arm and raised her hand in front of her, spread the fingers, looked at the hollow of her palm where the lines traced an interlocked pattern.

Her hand was open, not clenched tight, trying to hold on. And anything can come into an open hand. She let go and instead of empty, her hand was full. Of everything in the world.

"Barb?"

It was Sully, waking her up to go back to Cloud Peaks. She grunted as she got up and her neck was stiff. She helped him pack up and told him about the wolf.

"It probably wasn't a wolf. Sounds like a coyote." Barb didn't agree. It would always be a wolf to her.

Sully dismantled the tent, stowed everything in canvas packs and tied them on the horses. Then he led her back down the path, and Karen had saved some lunch for them.

"How did it go, Kimosabe?" Karen asked. She sat with them at the long dining table as they attacked a plate of sandwiches.

"Fantastic."

"Anything exciting?"

"I ran off a wolf, I mean, a coyote." Then Barb told her what happened.

"Pretty gutsy for a dude lady," said Sully.

"Not bad for an old broad," Barb replied. And they both grinned.

Barb had missed Christmas in July. Sully told her about the turkey, the oyster stuffing, sweet potatoes, green beans, relishes, pumpkin and mincemeat pies. She had a moment of regret, since she knew how good the cook was, but she was glad she had done what she had. The guests were busy and happy and Karen and Kirt kept things humming smoothly. They seemed easy together and Barb thought they must have worked out the Linda problem.

That afternoon Barb showered and went straight to the typewriter and tore up the Kate Chopin article. She marked paragraphs to save and put a fresh sheet in the typewriter and started again. The dinner bell caught her in midsentence. She stood and stretched. She'd stop now because she knew what she wanted to say next and it would be easy to start tomorrow. She walked to dinner with that heady satisfaction of having gone flat out all afternoon. She could barely collect her thoughts for dinner conversation. She excused herself early and was asleep before dark.

The next morning and the next—she lost track of how many days—she left the resort as soon as it was light and walked into the mountains. Sometimes she stayed in sight of the lake or the Cloud Peaks buildings. She was afraid she'd get lost and have to be sought like some heedless child, troubling Karen and the people at the resort. One time she walked down the road to a meadow and watched the neighbor's cows. One time she climbed rocks until her hands hurt and wouldn't hold. Most times she walked up a horse trail until she found a place, usually where there was a vista. Sometimes she wanted to be enclosed in the forested hills.

Some days she stayed out barely an hour, others she was out till noon. Each day, when she got back, she worked. After she set the Chopin article aside to cool off, she started another on dudes in Wyoming, beginning with Owen Wister's journal. She wrote press releases for Cloud Peaks, typed out a list of publications, and set a schedule of winter mailings. She worked on lecture outlines. She didn't keep up with the news, didn't want to know how high the Dow went or who was in the news. When she returned to Chopin, she realized she had enough for a book. She bled off the promised journal article and blocked in chapters. She went through notes and Xeroxes and earlier drafts, clipping papers to the chapter outlines. After half an hour she switched from paper clips to heavy art clamps. When she finished, she had the whole book outlined, with every reference and source where it belonged.

She still had to write the thing, but now she could put together a proposal and try to find a publisher. She had come to the end of a run.

She knew she could call Hal. She didn't have to fret about pleasing him or about whether he'd leave. She didn't need him, exactly. She wanted some company, wanted to get away from Cloud Peaks for a while. She could think about Marty without pain now, so she didn't need Hal to keep those hurts away. She wanted to be with him for the give-and-take of friendship.

She wondered what Hal was doing. What kind of horse was he shoeing? Where was he driving in those brown, sage-spotted hills? What music did he play on the pickup's tape deck? Which shirt was he wearing? Had he bashed another place raw on his rough hands? How was his bad meatloaf leg? Had his ex-wife and little girl come back to Casper?

Then she thought she could love him for what he was and know she didn't have to grab for his strength or worry she'd snap back like a rubber band.

She picked up the phone.

"You have reached Hal Simmons's number. I'm not here right now, but if you'll leave your name and number, I'll get back with you as soon as I can."

The sound of his familiar voice, always higher than she expected, warmed her, but she didn't know what to say.

"This is Barb Door," she said tentatively. "I want to see you. Call me at Cloud Peaks." She wanted to talk to him and have a drink and didn't know if there would be more to it than that. She only knew it was time and that words would be hard to find.

That night after dinner Karen called Barb to the phone.

"This is Hal, returning your call."

She couldn't speak. The quick retort, the snappy repartee was gone.

"Hello?" Hal's voice was a warm caress.

"Hi." She'd always talked tough. It covered up the scare. She felt all right, but didn't know a different way to be yet. "How are you?"

"Fine. Where've you been?"

"Camping, then here. How long since I left?"

There was a pause. "Couple of weeks."

"I lost track of time," she said. "How's your leg?"

"Fine. Still three colors, but it's okay." There was a laugh in his voice.

"I've been inside my own head too long. I want to see you." Not need to.

"Are we friends or lovers or buddies?" he asked.

"Do I have to decide?"

"No." He laughed, then so did she. "I've only got a small job tomorrow morning. Why don't you come down? I'll be back at the trailer by noon."

"I'll bring something for lunch."

24

Lars, the Cloud Peaks cook, made a stew with hot Italian sausage, mushrooms, onions, celery, carrots, and zucchini, lots of zucchini in August. It was hearty—loaded with garlic and oregano—and Hal and Barb mopped the last of the sauce with the wholewheat rolls. She poured herself a cup of coffee.

Hal's double-wide felt like home. She'd always thought trailers would feel crowded, with small rooms and low ceilings, but these rooms weren't badly proportioned. Hal furnished his with books and only a few pieces of furniture, so she never felt cramped. The old brown shag carpeting was worn almost through in front of the door and the couch was terminally threadbare. He kept it clean, but the big, slow Wyoming flies found their way inside. At first she swatted them frantically, but she'd gotten used to them and knew she'd never kill them all anyway.

"Then I slept outside the rest of the night. I knew it was irrational, but there you are. And it was funny, because I'd never have seen the stars if I hadn't. God, I thought I'd drown. There were millions more stars than I've ever seen before. It wasn't just that the air is clear and I was higher—I felt closer to them."

"Why didn't you just leave?" Hal asked.

"Something interesting might happen."

"Did it?" Hal pulled a can of beer out of the fridge and popped it.

"Yes."

"So?"

"A feeling that I died and came back to life."

"Sounds awful," he said, and swigged.

"No, it was wonderful. And frightening." She didn't think she could ever find words for it. "What have you been doing?"

"Same as usual. Working steady, keeping up with the paperwork."

"You don't need a secretary?" she asked.

"I don't need for you to be one," he answered.

"How's your leg?" She saw again the first-morning meat loaf, and shivered.

"Better," he said.

"Better than what?"

"Better than waking me up every four hours when the aspirin wears off."

"Good." She felt excited and hesitant, and didn't know what to say.

"So what does this all mean?" he asked.

"I don't know."

"You do a lot of things you don't know."

"At least this time I didn't hurt anybody or act stupid. That's something."

"Karen said you were hiking every day."

"When did you talk to her?"

"I came up to take care of the horses and you were gone."

"She didn't tell me." Barb was pleased and touched.

"She invited me for 'Christmas' dinner."

"Why didn't you come?"

"I didn't want to interfere. I thought I'd wait and let you work it out."

"I was gone that day anyway, but that makes me feel good to know you cared enough to ask her."

He sipped the Coors. She inhaled the winy coffee vapor. A pottery bowl sat on the Formica countertop. Browns streaked up from the base into blues near the rim, like Wyoming mountains and sky.

"I don't know what happened," she said. "I was afraid of the mountains, they weren't paved and predictable."

"So what did you do?"

"I went camping. Scared off the wolf, I mean the coyote. Faced being alone. I felt, feel really good. Then since I got back I've been working like crazy. When I gave up trying to find the other half of the coin, I had lots of energy. I sort of meditate, but it's not anything you can put a name to. I just go out and look, really look at the plants and rocks and birds."

"Good therapy." His eyes paled as the afternoon sun spread a parallelogram across the living-room floor. The pupils contracted and the iris blue washed out.

"I've been thinking about how to go back home," she said, "go to work, live alone. I kept grabbing for some ideas, some recipe. There aren't any. We make it up as we go along."

"And if it doesn't work?"

"Wait till these bootstrap burns on my hands heal and write a second draft." She grinned. She punched him lightly on the arm. "Or a third. I can write as many tries as I need to make it work." A laugh bubbled out.

"You sound good." He was grinning and his eyes held hers. "This was what you needed to do?"

"I think so. I don't know the answers, but I know they're out there."

She went to the couch and put her feet up on the battered coffee table. Two books lay facedown—*The Blind Corral* and a book on computer software.

"I thought of the women I know at home who seem happy. They're the ones with friends and interests aside from their work, although most of them are passionate about their professions. They have people, not necessarily children or husbands or lovers, to care about. When I go back, I'll be a better friend. People I didn't have much time for because Marty took up my time. A pair of season tickets to the opera and the symphony, so I'll have to ask someone to go with me."

"That sounds good. Like you won't fall back in the trap without knowing it."

"I know it just doesn't happen once and you turn into a different person. I'll have to cycle through it over and over, the way I cycled through the hurt after Grimaldi left. But I can remember what happened and know I can get through whatever comes. And I can remember the waterfall."

The parallelogram crept across the floor. The midday light was blinding. Hal got up and twisted the miniblinds closed, then limped over to join her on the couch. "Are you going to be a hermit all summer?"

"What day is it?" She really had lost track of time.

"The first of August."

"Less than three weeks left." She stretched and thought. "I've really been whaling away at my preps. This will be the best class I've ever done. I've finished the lecture notes. I can't wait to get back. Those articles are coming along. Did I tell you I think I've got a book—at least it looks like I've got enough ideas for one?" They sat in companionable silence for long moments. Then Barb asked, "Can I come back?"

"Of course." He put an arm around her shoulders. "What do you want?"

"I want to make love, of course." She grinned and gave him a peck on the cheek. "But I want something else. I fell for your funny conversation and your hard body and that hat and those boots. You look the part."

"Of what?"

"The cowboy hero. The western dream."

"All the time I thought you loved me for myself."

"I want to know the Hal behind my fantasy projection. You told me about your divorce and your little girl and I started to learn more. I can't love you if I don't know you."

"Do I have to go through that again?"

"I didn't mean for you to be unhappy," she said.

"No, I needed to look at what happened and face it."

"This has been a 'face it' time for both us."

"Well, what now?"

"I can think of something."

She wrapped her arms around him and leaned forward to kiss the back of his neck—brown and clean and strong. The gray-threaded hair grew around his ears, curling a little. She brushed it back so she could run her tongue around the rosy edge of one ear. She wanted to make love to Hal, the person. Not her idea of him. Not the cowboy image of boots and hat and outdoor tan.

"Let's be loving friends," she said. "I think I can love you without sucking your blood."

"Ouch."

"That's all right. I know I'll have to leave. I won't try to hold on and strangle us. If I slip, you'll remind me."

They got up from the couch and embraced. It was a friendly hug for a long time. Then his arms dropped and he cupped her ass and pulled her against his erection. She felt the muscles defined through his cotton shirt, the half-buried line of his spine, and rested her face to breathe the hollow of his collarbone. She kissed him and one of them groaned.

His bedroom smelled like sun and fresh sheets. He stripped her out of her clothes, then pushed her gently until she sat on the edge of the bed.

He skinned out of his shirt, she pulled off his boots, and he shucked off his jeans. He stood there like some mountain she could never know. She could trace the veins up the insides of his arms and learn the topography of his back and memorize the moles on his shoulder and test the clean smell of his skin, but she couldn't know him.

She was bewildered. She knew his past and his kindness and his body and his loving. She could live with him fifty years and never know the secret life in his mind, all that he was. She couldn't hold him or take him to Kansas City or pretend she understood him. He was a mystery as profound as the rocks and the flowers and the wind.

She let go and opened her arms to him.

25

In August Barb flew down the mountain from Cloud Peaks ready for the weekend. She waited for Hal at his trailer, and after they made love, they sketched out the weekend. There were polo games on Sundays. One weekend there was the Basque fair in Buffalo, another the county rodeo in Sheridan. In Buffalo, the old high school was coming down, and dust and noise from up the hill drifted around the pool where they swam. They stopped at the twelve-foot chain-link that surrounded the building and saw tanned, hard-muscled men in caps and broad-brimmed hats with mallets and jackhammers. She wondered if they were Jim Bobs.

One Friday night there was a clambake at Porky's Bar in Ucross. They drove east from Buffalo as the sun went down behind them. Wild turkeys scattered from the shoulder of the highway. They passed a few pickups that sat at the edge of a little reservoir east of the interstate. The rounded hills covered with sparse grass repeated again and again as they drove. Uncut alfalfa was a lavender haze in the irrigated pastures. Huge loaf-shaped rolls of hay edged fields where the machines had stopped at sunset.

Ucross: elevation 4,000 feet, population 25. There were three or four times that many people inside the country bar and outside on the concrete around the gas pumps. They got there in time to taste the last of the clams.

"Where did they get the clams?" Barb asked, suspicious that they wouldn't be fresh.

"Through Tunnel Inn in Story," said one of the men helping himself to potato salad, bread, and hamburger sloppy joes.

They ate, and about nine, members of the three-piece combo of bass, lead guitar, and drums mounted a platform at one end of the concrete in front of Porky's. The middle-aged musicians were solid and competent and enjoyed what they did. She and Hal danced for a while, then took a break for beer and he began talking to man who needed a farrier. Barb watched the residents from the artists' colony creep timidly from their house across the way. They talked owlishly among themselves until their keeper, a dour blond youngster, and his friend, the smiling innocent Ucross Foundation worker they'd seen mowing grass, introduced them to the painter from Story and the senator's son who was a writer. Hal grabbed the painter, a dark-haired woman Barb's age, for the butterfly. It was a folk-type dance in which one man and two women did a set of steps, then do-si-doed as the big circle of dancers moved around the gas pumps. The music was slow for the set steps, then went wild as they wove from hand to hand in a little circle, racing to keep up with the music.

After that, when Barb was talking to Vira, she heard a man who sounded just like Curry Cannon. She turned quickly to see, but it was another cleancut, well-pressed cowboy from the Ucross ranch making up to a pretty, blond girl in a stylish baggy sweatshirt and sprayed-on jeans. Barb and Hal danced and she was glad she was dancing with him instead of doing something stupid with Curry or someone like him.

She talked to a woman in a coral sweater whose husband worked for the huge corporation that dominated the area. "We get our housing and beef and all benefits," she told Barb, "but not as much money. It works out about the same."

"It sounds like feudalism," Barb said. The woman shrugged and said it worked.

Later the manager of Porky's announced the catfish were ready. The cook had filled a new galvanized garbage can with water, spices, onions, whole potatoes, and catfish and boiled it all together. It tasted better than it sounded.

They danced and drank beer and talked until the band quit, then they joined the pickups kicking gravel as they spun out of Porky's parking lot.

She got out her parka and bought gloves and scarves at the Custom Cowboy and walked the mountain around Cloud Peaks in the cold, pearly August rain. A couple of mornings there was a dusting of snow that melted before noon. She gathered silver gray-green sage. Its clean smell was Wyoming and she wanted to take a little home. It was astringent, almost sharp, and the cleanest smell she'd ever known.

Then came that day in August when she had to leave. She and Karen said a tearful good-bye as Barb loaded her station wagon with more papers than she'd brought and a Stetson hatbox.

"Come and visit me in Kansas City," said Barb. She felt awkward and fumbled for words. "Thanks for helping me put my life back together. Thanks for giving me this place to do it."

Karen shrugged. Barb saw the years of affection brim in Karen's eyes and felt her own tears overflow. "I wasn't a very good friend to you when you and Kirt were having trouble."

"I knew you were on my side. That was enough." Karen's fair skin blotched red as she cried. Barb knew she was red-eyed herself.

Karen looked around the resort. "Our summer is almost over, too. The last guests leave next weekend. Then a business-meeting weekend and we close up for another year. I'm always glad to come up here at the start of summer and sad to leave in September. While I'm in the middle of everything I don't think about it. I should just stop and enjoy it more."

They walked to the reservoir for one last sunset. "I hope it all doesn't wash away when you get back," Karen said. "Are you going to be all right? You'll have to face Marty and the Croatian bride and everybody."

"I think the Wyoming cure will transfer." Barb hugged her, then they walked to the edge of the gleaming water. She could think of Grimaldi's sunset alerts without pain. She remembered Tony and the first time she'd walked out here and wept. Sunsets when she camped. Sunsets through the windows of Hal's trailer.

Blue-bordered clouds took color from the sun, that ruddy color of Wyoming earth, streaked with shades of pink and amethyst and violet and lavender and rose and crimson and orange and vermillion. The line just above the peak of the mountain was pure light, then the palette rioted until the sky darkened into night and the stars came.

After Barb said good-bye to Karen and they'd hugged one last time, she drove to Hal's trailer, taking presents—books on computers and a package of boxer shorts from Pamida. Tapes of Mozart, Vaughan Williams, Willie Nelson, and Jerry Jeff Walker, Nakai, Bob Marley, and U2. He surprised her with an amber pendant on a heavy gold chain.

"Something from the earth," he said. The big, polished chunk lay heavy and warm in her hand. She studied the inclusions of air bubbles, a bit of leaf, and an insect, perfectly preserved.

Barb bustled around the trailer, returned a borrowed shirt, handkerchiefs, books. She found one of her blouses in his closet and checked his dresser for her lingerie. Hal sat on the couch, his legs on the coffee table, watching her.

"Slow down," he said.

She stopped. "Trying to stay busy," she said. "So I don't think about leaving."

"You *are* leaving."

"There, you went and said it." She stumbled to the couch and burrowed under his arm.

"You can run, pilgrim, but you can't hide," he murmured.

Running mascara soaked into the pointed yoke of his shirt.

"Don't you think I want you to stay?"

"I needed to hear it," she said.

He stroked her hair. "We knew it wouldn't last."

"I knew that. But it doesn't mean it doesn't hurt now." When she twisted around, she saw that his eyes were sad. Their blue had soaked up the misery and turned dark.

"D'you remember that bronze bronco rider on the mantel at the Bradford Brinton museum?" he asked. "By Charlie Russell? A moment frozen. Every detail worked out and perfect. Well, this summer is like one of those statues. It's just this moment and the moment will pass and things will change. Russell's cowboy has lost his stirrup and he's going flying. The summer is ending." He cradled her to him. "That doesn't mean we can't get together some other time, some other place. I don't know if this computer business will succeed. If Julie marries her fiancé, she'll take Mary Louise to live in California. I'd only get her in the summertime."

"But you'd be her all-summer daddy."

"Maybe I'll move to Kansas City."

"It's a great place to raise kids." Barb paused. "You deflected," she said.

"Yes." He took a deep breath. "It feels like a stone in my chest. If it hurt like my leg, I'd know what to do. I just keep thinking the weight will go away. And it doesn't."

"You said once I could be anything I wanted in

Buffalo County, Wyoming, even myself. I said I'd try it if I could figure out who I was. I've got a better idea now. I'm not looking for the other half of the coin." She looked at his sad face. "Thanks for being patient when I was acting impossible."

"I should thank you. I haven't been involved with a woman, not seriously, since Julie walked out. You've made me think it's worth the grief."

She punched his arm. "Thanks a bunch."

"No, no." He laughed. "I didn't realize I was scared to try again. Now I have and it's been great." He looked away and she knew he wasn't seeing the bookcase opposite the couch. "I once said we expect more from women in Wyoming. You took it wrong. But in a way you showed me what you're made of—a little bad and a lot good. Loving, friendly. A little mystical. Gutsy."

"Thanks. That embarrasses me."

"What I'm trying to say is, I'll miss you so much I don't know how I'll stand it."

His arms tightened around her and she held him as hard as she could. She couldn't seem to stop crying. It wasn't sobbing and carrying on, it was just steady tears, as though she overflowed with sadness.

"The hardest thing," she said, "is that I won't be a part of your life."

"You'll always be a part of my life, pilgrim."

"No, I mean like you and Mary Louise—doing everyday things, knowing when she loses a tooth or what she wore to school that day. I won't be able to share those homely things—like knowing where you're working or if you need help taking a shower."

"You almost fainted that time," he teased.

"I never faint."

"You turned a funny color of green."

"Anyway, you know what I mean. I hope I can come back here or you can visit me. Probably when we see each other, we'll take up where we left off, like me and Karen. But it won't be rubbing your shoulders when you're tired or listening when you cuss out some client's horse."

"Yes, I know what you mean." He brushed her hair back from her face and touched a rough finger to her nose. "I can't learn the rhythm of your days. I'll miss making love with you, but I'll miss talking to you more." He kissed her softly, then pulled her into a hard hug. She couldn't see his face, but felt his warm, moist breath in her ear. "I'll miss the way you smell, and watching your eyes cross when we make love. I'll miss watching that tense look fade after you've been with me for a while." He sniffed as though his nose were running. "And I'll miss knowing what your new boyfriend is like."

"Oh, you think I'll get a boyfriend?"

"Inevitable. Just don't try too hard."

"I'll try not to let thinking of you get in the way—I'll miss your hair pasted to your forehead under your hat, your rough hands. The taste of your skin. Your weight on me." Then she had to stop. She blew her nose some more. "I'll keep coming back to Wyoming every summer, that funny dude lady who brings her typewriter."

"Come back," he choked. "Maybe one of these times I'll go home with you."

"Or I'll decide to stay."

He squeezed and she squeezed back and she

COMING NEXT MONTH

SILVER SHADOWS by Marianne Willman

In this dramatic western of love and betrayal, Marianne Willman, author of *Yesterday's Shadows,* continues the saga of the Howards. Intent on revenge for wrongs done to his family, half-Cheyenne Grayson Howard unexpectedly finds love with a beautiful widow.

THE WAY IT SHOULD HAVE BEEN by Georgia Bockoven

From the author of *A Marriage Of Convenience* comes a story of drama, courage, and tenderness. Carly is reasonably happy with a stable marriage and three wonderful children. Then David comes back to town. Now a famous author, David had left twenty years before when Carly married his best friend. He'd never stopped loving Carly, nor forgiven her for leaving him. Yet, Carly did what she had to do. It was the only way to keep the secret she must hide—at all costs.

THE HEART'S LEGACY by Barbara Keller

When Céline Morand married the man she'd dreamed of for years, she thought the demands of love and duty were the same. But an unexpected trip to the lush plantation of her husband's cousin in Louisiana ends Céline's naiveté and opens her heart to a man she can't have.

LADY OF LOCHABAR by Jeanette Ramirez

In this beautiful, heartbreaking love story, Maggie Macdonald is but seven years old when Simon Campbell saves her life after his father's army has massacred her entire family. As fate would have it, they meet ten years later and enter into a forbidden love.

OUT OF THE PAST by Shirl Jensen

When Debbie Dillion moves to Texas to pick up the pieces of her life, she finds her dream house waiting for her. But soon Debbie wonders if she has walked into a living nightmare, where someone is willing to do anything to hide the past—even commit murder.

WHEN DESTINY CALLS by Suzanne Elizabeth

A delightful time-travel romance about a modern-day police officer, Kristen Ford, who would go to any distance—even to the rugged mountains of Nevada in the 1890s—to find her soul mate.

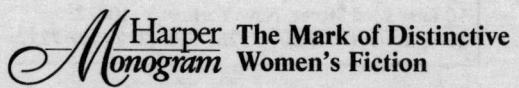

Harper Monogram The Mark of Distinctive Women's Fiction

ATTENTION: ORGANIZATIONS AND CORPORATIONS

Most HarperPaperbacks are available at special quantity discounts for bulk purchases for sales promotions, premiums, or fund-raising. For information, please call or write:
Special Markets Department, HarperCollins Publishers,
10 East 53rd Street, New York, N.Y. 10022.
Telephone: (212) 207-7528. Fax: (212) 207-7222.

HarperPaperbacks By Mail

If you like romance, passion and adventure, you're sure to like these...

4 Unforgettable Romantic Love Stories

These four novels are filled with intrigue and suspense and overflow with love, passion and romance.

PRIDE OF PLACE by Nicola Thorne. Judith Prynne sees the opportunity of a lifetime. Follow her from London to all of Europe, in a passionate quest for money, power and the love of a man who could take it all away.

THE HOUSE OF VANDEKAR by Evelyn Anthony. A family dynasty struggles for five decades against its two obsessions: love and betrayal. They wove an intricate web of love and lies that trapped them all.

A TIME TO SING by Sally Mandel. Fate brought them together and bonded their hearts in a dreamed-of perfect life. Then fate returns and tries to take it all away. This is a story of star crossed love that you will never forget.

SPRING MOON by Bette Bao Lord. Spring Moon was born into luxury and privilege. Through a tumultuous lifetime, Spring Moon must cling to her honor, to the memory of a time gone by and to a destiny, foretold at her birth, that has yet to be fulfilled.

Buy All 4 and $ave. When you buy all four the postage and handling is *FREE*. You'll get these novels delivered right to door with absolutely no charge for postage, shipping and handling.

Visa and MasterCard holders—call 1-800-331-3761 for fastest service!

MAIL TO: Harper Collins Publishers, P. O. Box 588, Dunmore, PA 18512-0588, Tel: (800) 331-3761

YES, send me the love stories I have checked:

☐ **Pride Of Place**
0-06-100106-6....$4.95

☐ **The House Of Vandekar**
0-06-100050-7....$4.95

☐ **A Time To Sing**
0-06-100066-3...$4.95

☐ **Spring Moon**
0-06-100105-8....$4.95

SUBTOTAL.............................$_____

POSTAGE AND HANDLING*............$_____

SALES TAX (NJ, NY, PA residents).........$_____

Remit in US funds, do not send cash   **TOTAL:** $_____

Name_____

Address_____

City_____

State_____Zip_____ Allow up to 6 weeks delivery. Prices subject to change.

*Add $1 postage/handling for up to 3 books...**FREE postage/handling if you buy all 4.**

H0051

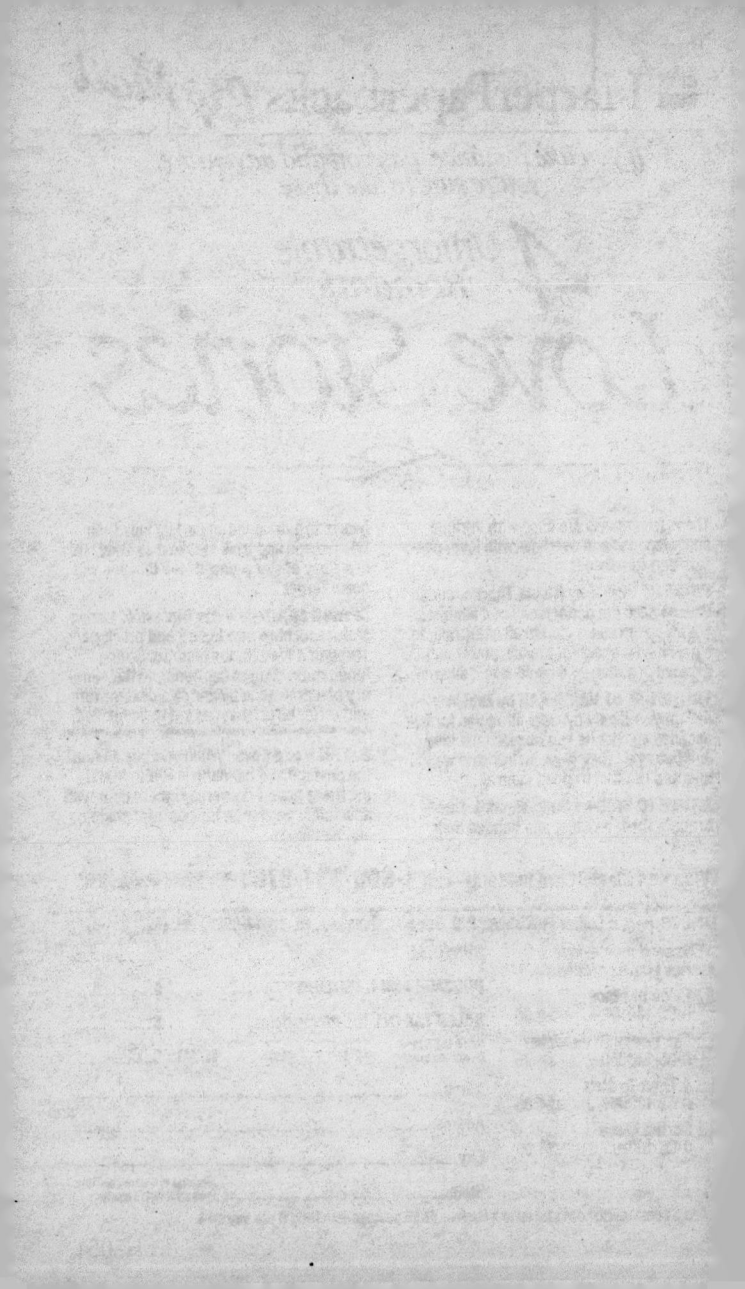